Thomas Lake Harris

Conversation in Heaven

A Wisdom Song

Thomas Lake Harris

Conversation in Heaven
A Wisdom Song

ISBN/EAN: 9783337001599

Printed in Europe, USA, Canada, Australia, Japan

Cover: Foto ©Andreas Hilbeck / pixelio.de

More available books at **www.hansebooks.com**

CONVERSATION IN HEAVEN

A WISDOM SONG

BY

THOMAS LAKE HARRIS

———————

" Did not our hearts burn within us
while He talked with us by the way."
LUKE XXIV. 32.

———————

FOUNTAINGROVE
Privately Printed
1894.

DEDICATORY EPISTLE.

TO

W.   R.

STANDING to-day upon Time's utmost peak,
   As the discoverer once on Darien,
The great south seas upon the vision break,
   The timeless Life World rounding to my ken.
Truth is made on-sight; each low wave, that swells
To break beneath the feet, a mystery tells.

Etheric roll the waters heaving far,
   All musical in wisdom's measured flow,
Breathing to melodies that pregnant are
   With the New Life that folds us to bestow.
Through each impregnate sense take form and wing
Swift revelations; to the heart they sing.

Now, as my bosom draws the blithe, warm wind
   That leads me on the Godlands to explore,
I waft such strains of poesies behind
   As serve to guide the feet to find the "Door,"
And show the "Way," that opens for release
To Isles of Blessedness in seas of peace.

"Sweetheart," spake one who claims and comforts me,
  "A friend is at the call who feels akin."
I opened and a Pilgrim, gallantly
  Equipped for daring travel, ventured in.
Beholding him as "Christian" I inclined ;
Thence we embraced by sympathies entwined.

'Twas Bunyan of the "Progress"; now he dwells
  In England's Heaven and is a Bishop there.
Upon mine ears grew chime of wedding bells ;
  The one oped full to twain, right blessed pair.
"Christian" and "Christiana" one-in-twain,
John Bunyan and his lady, beamed amain.

Spake they in union, trumpet toned in lute,
  "Thou wert in Britain but the other day
And clasped one there, a godly soul in fruit,
  Whose heart in thine and ours makes warm array :
Bid him God cheer."—William, of this I tell
And dedicate the Song to thee as well.

PART FIRST

—

"Our Conversation is in Heaven ; from whence also we look for the Savior, the Lord Jesus Christ: who shall change our vile body, that it may be fashioned like unto His glorious body, according to the working whereby He is able even to subdue all things unto Himself."

PHIL. III. 20, 21.

CONVERSATION IN HEAVEN.

—

1

UPLIFT, New Man, uplift in exultation ;
  Time's utmost mountain peak at last is scaled.
Breasting all wraths, wrought to one desolation,
  Thou in God burdened hast by Him prevailed.
Lift orient brow, full-bosomed meet the sun :
Hail the new morn ; breathe full with heaven at-one.

2

Height,length and breadth, these shape the third dimension.
  · Thou hast o'ercome, outfilled, transcended all :
Thine is the throughness, organized extension,
  The wondrous fourth: — reflect, repeat, recall ;
Collect thy thought in God through nature's round
And time's abyss and mystery's dim profound.

3

The path of Throughness opens : lo! the gates
  Of the eternal are for touch ajar.
'Tis the concentered soul that contemplates,
  As through its system thinks the solar star.
In the low minors of the opening third
Pulse the freed octaves of the four-fold Word.

II.

1

"Man's an intelligence whom organs serve,"
    Aquinas reasoned in his syllogism.
Follow the thought to the dimension's curve ;
    View it illumined in the mental prism.
The quickened man, by feeling, thought and sense,
Is organ for the Word's Intelligence.

2

The sentient crystal of the universe
    Is human ; its live molecules are men.
Organs they are through whom the rays disperse
    From the True Light and flow to light again ;
Yet those alone are men who feed on light
And by it thrive and for its ends unite.

3

An atheist as to Theosocialism,
    Though seeming man, is but a shade, a shell,
Whose hollow self builds up its blind abysm
    With magic forms grouped by an evil spell,
And so is compassed with illusive gleams
Whereof it rears the systems of its dreams.

4

He is a creature of enormous toil,
    And yet of all the creatures most infirm.
Holding by organs in a triune coil,
    Three-score and ten is their persistent term.
Though he by strength should linger past four-score,
Death sounds his 'larum peal from door to door.

III.

1

All sacred gifts await their opportune.
  The crowning gifts of God's new time await
Till feeling, thought and sense in perfect tune
  Out-lift the organs through their three-fold state.
The third dimension holds the worm in plan;
The fourth holds God, in fashion as the Man.

2

Think to the fourth; think faithly if at all.
  In the out-lift alone are safeties found.
To think the third as final is to fall
  In sheer abasement to non-human ground.
Faith leads the evolution from the mesh
Of pictured nature to the Word made flesh.

3

The third is all a matrix and therein
  True man from seed of Word shapes on to grow;
Height, length and breadth by formal style to win;
  Weaving the outness of his being so.
Phrased in the natural scripture by his third,
He fills its content from his Cause, the Word.

4

And this is life, true life, that he may know
  His God incarnate to extreme of needs,
And put on God in fourths, and own Him so,
  And follow God in throughness, whence proceeds
The pathway of pure being, made complete
Where, in the Infinite, all finites meet.

5

Think thou to God to lead thy throughness on :
  Think that the forms that serve Him may transpose :
Think of thy being, made a daughter-son
  And led to new beginnings from the close :
Think of thy form transcendent o'er the strife ;
Throughness led forth by all the doors of life.

6

So is " Captivity led captive " ; so
  Death, "the last enemy," for thee shall fail,
Dissolving in life's victory.   The flow
  Of God in throughness rounds the mighty scale
Of life's triumphant harmonies ; they blend
For the "new song," the song without an end.

IV.

1

There was a MAN who stood in Paradise :
  All names of worth are His in one great name.
Morning shone forth from His illustrious eyes.
  He spake, "By throughness unto thee I came,
And with thee in this new dimension stand,
That I may show thee of the glorious land."

2

Then came forth ladies, matrons virginal,
  Led by divine processions through His form ;
For He is made their dwelling, and the wall
  Of their perfections.   Blithe and sweet and warm
They wove a dance of hymeneal choirs ;
Then entered Him again by loves in fires.

3

Thence issued knights, bridegrooms of such pure brides,
　　And lo! the Man, now Woman, beamed to greet
Their righteousness.　As waves to ocean glide,
　　Melodious, worshipful they met Her feet.
Soon, as their prayer-song found a blissful close,
They entered Her. drawn on to love's repose.

4

Such follow Thee, our Lord! where'er Thou goest,
　　For they abide in and come forth from Thee;
And as the ocean Thou to fill them flowest:
　　Thou art to them dimension, and the sea
Of crystalline clear fire, by zone in zone,
Tides from Thy shining as an orbed white throne.

V.

1

Grasped in the infamy of life's repression,
　　Earth's wasted peoples generate. disease:
For immanation they have wrought obsession:
　　For emanation wrathful tyrannies;
A scientific magic; the "black art"
Bred·by the false mind in the evil heart.

2

As in the rivers minnows are to pikes,
　　So on earth's range true saints to sinners are.
The man who smites not, to the churl who strikes,
　　As crystal mirror meets the iron bar.
The evil harden on, blow after blow;
The good grow sensitive by worth in flow.

3

The third dimension, as it narrows in,
    Contracts upon the generous ardent soul.
Magic has wrought a wilderness of sin,
    Spaced in illusions that the sense control.
Mind, that would fourth dimensioned truths declare,
Meets death in life, obstruction everywhere.

4

" Earth is the limbo of the universe,"
    Spake Fourier, Wisdom vocal on his lips.
Her chariot of ascension shapes to hearse :
    Time is for her the shade of an eclipse.
God is eclipsed, God is eclipsed in man ;
Self,—the gorged self-snake,—rules the three-fold plan.

5

"Subversive evolution,"—note it well,—
    This other fact of earthly time he said.
Man, failing to shape heaven, creates his hell.
    Earth at the chariot wheels of death is led,
A chained, dumb captive, urged by terrors on
To cataclysm and oblivion.

6

" Impenetrable ignorance, this plea
    May save the soul from an eternal pain " :
Thus Rome by a remains of charity
    Holds hope to man when other hopes were vain.
Upon this generation, lingering yet
Anigh the fated verge, such seal is set.

7

Its ears are closed so that it cannot hear;
　Its eyes are seared so that it shall not see;
Its brain, grown hollow, is a shadowed sphere
　Where the heart's hardness shapes vacuity
To moving shapes, illusive, self-inwrought,
Not thought but lifeless images of thought.

8

The seed of God is stifled from the root,
　But for it spectral nature seed has grown.
Men breathe contagion from the dissolute
　Waste vapors, where the airy space is sown,
From the accurst impure magnetic dust
Of human ill, with microscopic lust.

9

Instead of God the swarmed bacteria come.
　Nature seven-fold has multiplied the curse
Man casts into her: now it makes an home
　In him and generates, so to asperse
The burdened organs, where he holds his breath,
With fetid rains of generative death.

10

Woe then to prophets, in this evil time
　Of prescient doom, who prophesy smooth things.
Woe to the seers who see no crime in crime,
　But progress climbing by ascensive rings.
Woe to the priests, when God holds open door
For coming truth, who cry "no more, no more!"

VI.

1

The mortal brain, made by suppression massive,
  Resists the ardors of the Vital Sun.
To base results grown by the self-will passive,
  Through all the reason, by result, is spun
A clinging surface, that obstructs the ray
Of wisdom's effluence from the Lord, our Day.

2

Yet day-break is upon us: would men open
  Senses to God as they to nature ope,
The bars of third dimension might be broken:
  Then in an hour the dark, wherein they grope,
Stumble and perish, melt to royal light,
So to restore the paradisal sight.

3

Millions there are who grope and stumble so:
  All days hold pit-falls and all nights are snares:
The third dimension will not have them go:
  Conflicts unknown inexplicable theirs;
For throughness, urging on to motions free,
Is girt by anarchy and tyranny.

4

Thus the last struggle centers in the brain.
  The fourth dimensioned mind its organ forms,
But growing on, its lucid orb to gain,
  Shapes its new motion through resistant storms:
Each sympathetic nerve is grasped in strain.—
Hold faithly now; hold to the Lord One-Twain.

5

Here is Religion's last annunciation :
   Lord Christus claims the mortal battle field ;
By immanation moves to emanation :
   Speeds on to evidence, our Sun and Shield.
The fourth dimension, rounding through the third.
Makes nature all an out-field for the Word.

VII.

1

The fourth is nothing if not practical ;
   'Tis order, law and service everywhere ;
No place therein to dally or to fall.
   'Tis Theosocialism fills the air ;
Heart led through heart and hand led free through hand ;
All throughnesses in throughness of God's land.

2

Upon the fact of throughness, interunion,
   Pivots the wheel that fashions all the space.
Feeling, thought, passion, in divine communion
   Through all to each, find freedom and embrace.
Repose and action are as night and day,
All march of sun-force and all stars in play.

3

I saw a king, on earth a Methodist,
   The founder of such service, and he said,
"I Wesley was ; here twain-one I persist,
   Fulfilling that whereto my life was led
When, in the wilds of labor-time below,
I thought to plant for God and have it grow.

4

"Now here, behold, is God-wrought Methodism
   In fourth dimension : to its kingdom feel.
Stript of the limitations that make schism,
   I serve as pivot of its social wheel.
The fourth, to the extreme in God, its wall,
Is one in many kingdoms, each in all."

5

A man of deeds, a Priest Napoleon,
   I read in Wesley to his Word-filled heart ;
Read him in fact as now a king, twain-one
   By inter-throughness with his counterpart.
'Tis through Religion, by its work of grace,
Kingdoms are nurtured for celestial space.

6

True growth depends on order for its wheel :
   On ordered growth all human good depends :
The laws of order in' their course reveal
   The paths of order to creation's ends :
The ends of order in result display
The Word Twain-One, the Life, the Truth, the Way.

7

'Tis so mankind escapes its limitations ;
   By throughness finds the infinite career ;
Led by continuous and discrete gradations,
   Throughness in throughness opening sphere by sphere.
Man, who in order to result has trod,
Dwells by full consciousness in God with God.

8

Only the thorough may attain to throughness.
  "Do what thou hast to do with all thy might";
Move on thereby in the eternal newness,
  Led so to victory from sight to sight.
"No age makes impotent, no custom stales";
The infinite variety prevails.

9

The third dimension lastly satiates;
  It keeps no final good for man in store.
The joy stood tip-toe; through the opening gates
  It sped, to vanish and return no more:
The blissful cup, from lip to lip that passed,
But held and gave exhaustion at the last.

10

This is the bitterness that hides behind
  These mortal confines: Wordless shadows, dead
To all but life's appearance, merely find
  Their third dimension to its vapor spread.
To bleak old age, in impotency curled,
Coils the man ego in the under world.

VIII.

1

Come forth in this imperial warm July.
  The nation to the Twain-One bows no knee:
Constant it is to claim and glorify
  False ego's base non-human liberty:
It grinds as Egypt did the serfs to dust:
Its glaive is sharpened at the Word to thrust.

2

2

Its greatness is not substance, 'tis inflation,
　　Herculean pride that mounts before the fall :
Progress but seems. 'tis mere deterioration.
　　Now, woven through glad sunshine, floats a pall.
Falsehood and evil by rank commerce breed
Swarmed spores, upon all mortal flesh to feed.

3

Man's form of volatiles must lose cohesion :
　　"Dust that he is, to dust he shall return."
Organs, that ope by many a sightless lesion,
　　Hold secret wounds that bleed and weep and burn.
The fetid generations of the spore
Lead vegetative death from sore to sore.

4

Elijah had his ravens, and they fed him
　　All the dread years when baal's priests held sway.
The cave for shelter opened to bestead him,
　　Holding a shadow wrought for kindlier day.
The fourth dimension now gives open arms
To shield God's prophets from the last alarms.

5

Alone and still alone, amid the millions
　　Who throng the parks, the avenues and drives,
I hear the minstrels in the gay pavilions,
　　But see the worm that in the players thrives.
Reddens the gold that crowns on summer's brow,
But death is harvest that is ripening now.

6

Death has inclosed the planet, and it journeys
   Till all its multitudes in one are wound ;
Till all are as the fuel in the furnace ;
   Till all are pierced into their inmost ground,
And those who hold, from those who shun the fourth,
Severed as babes are from the after-birth.

7

Here is no hiding place ; all now who hide
   Must occultly in one vast plexus meet ;
All men to reach the cliffs of one divide ;
   All from the planet's brow unto its feet.
All men, all molecules of men, must feel
And turn and change when God is made the Wheel.

8

Heights of dimension, in surcharged increase,
   The ruinous and final fall precede ;
All breadths of empires sunder piece by piece
   To the last broken wall and moldering weed ;
All lengths of pleasures, at the fated spot,
Dissolve as empires fail and ages rot.

9

Now Judgment, as the Mother, calls to me,
   And I must sit within Her awful doors,
Till ends "the strange eventful history"
   Of time, and paradise its bloom restores ;
Till the new lengths and breadths and heights, concealed
In the Word's fourthness, show an open field.

IX.

1

Judgment, She sits apart in palace gardens,
    Throned in the true, the sacred, the sublime.
Her holiness from brow to feet She hardens
    To breast and penetrate resistant crime. '
Her lips, whereto God's lips their seal have set,
Hold silence; there the dews of sleep are met.

2

Silence and sleep! sure-stepping, sweet and saintly,
    Divine Night-Walker, in a wondrous dream,
Where the white stars like water-lilies faintly
    Ope their pale petals on the azure stream,
She keeps the ways of the mysterious round,
Circling the planet, feeling to its bound.

3

In the warm sun-sphere's glowing undulations
    She orbs Her presence as a lovelier moon.
The interstellar ether leads vibrations,
    Born of Her motion, to a low sweet tune,
A crooning melody, a flying charm
Touching the sense to soothe its last alarm.

4

As the brook's waters in a summer spate
    The broidered meadow banks may overbrim,
Judgment is gliding, kindly, delicate,
    Orbed in pure ether, wakening that sweet hymn;
Touching slow, surely, till by calm consent
All human lives in one repose are blent.

5

Come forth with me again while heavens dissolve
   A dewy tenderness: a manifold,
Ripe richness, that the pleasances evolve,
   Feeds the warm sense: men hearten blithe and bold.
Nature has donned the matron; she has pressed
All living creatures to her flowing breast.

6

Yet see! through all this bravery of apparel
   Nature is changing to another style.
Heights, lengths and breadths the peoples hold in quarrel.
   This is a weary time; beneath the smile
Of solar lips that kiss the toiling race
The secret pestilence makes eager pace.

X.

1

The Holiness of holiness displays
   Beauties from Beauty in Her hallowed mart.
Supreme arch-nature to its form arrays
   In the perfections of transcendent art.
By change on change from scene to scene we pass,
As living radiance through translucent glass.

2

"When the without shall be as the within
   The kingdom cometh"; so the Master spake,
Meaning the throughness, led the world to win,
   Throughness by throughness, till mankind awake;
While then the pure in heart, by faith who trod,
Shall put on heaven and "in their flesh see God."

3

Heaven crowds not on mankind as to encroach.
　By the full being in full play we move,
So keeping pace with the divine approach.
　Advance is in the sympathy of love ;
God feeling forth in us the more we feel,
Till, life in life, all lives His Life reveal.

XI.

1

The house wherein we dwell is moving: see!
　The interstellar ether breathes to fire :
The spirits of the atoms, wondrously
　As living sparks, within their orbs respire.
Feel to the motion ; feel and so behold ;
The new-born order turns upon the old.

2

The fourth dimension presses on the third
　That suffocates the just in living graves.
"To resurrection !" calls the Bridal Word,
　In power that thrills and liberates and saves.
It is the many who as one shall hear ;
Then through that manifold the Word appear.

3

Here is no tumult of the throbbing drums,
　No sounding of the bugles for parade.
Mute as the gathering snowfall Judgment comes :
　In Her white livery is the world arrayed.
The vast scene-curtain must remain intact
Till expectation merges in the act.

4

Men move with faces turned from one another.
  Judgment revealing shall the faces turn;
All Her elect, the world-wide sister-brother,
  Shall face to face with kindlier ardors burn,
And see one face beaming through all at-one,
God's face reflected through each daughter-son.

5

Men toil, worn swimmers in a ghastly torrent,
  Each striking out alone to breast the stroom.
The whirling waves, drawn to an upward current,
  Shall lift them glowing o'er the watery doom;
Lift them on Judgment's breast in time and tone
To Life's arisen land, their own, Her own.

6

Judgment involves man's fleshly particles:
  His atoms are in judgment and they know.
The third dimension's movement stuns or kills
  Man's apprehensive sense; he lieth low;
His prison overcomes him, and the maze
Of memory, and its labyrinthine ways.

7

Earth stands in Judgment and it knows it not:
  Earth looks in Judgment and no sights aver;
Learning, grown magical, from time would blot
  Faith's last lone spark lit in the sepulcher;
Yet there it swims aloft o'er trance and swoon,
Her sign in heaven, the cold, white Judgment moon.

XII.

1

The path of years is by a single thread,
   Like the tense nerve that spans Niagara's chasm.
Decisively in the brave prime we tread
   Till the worn line beneath us writhes in spasm.
The steps at last are timorous, feeble, slow :
One inadvertence leads the overthrow.

2

The round of years is by a breadth that narrows ;
   We fasten then like limpets to the rock.
Exultantly we raced as fiery arrows,
   Nor feared the piercing place, nor shunned the shock.
Foot fast and hand fast, narrowed to the cell,
Prisoned from spacial freedom we must dwell.

3

The rise of years is by an height that climbs
   Upward still upward ; perilous the steep.
Resistances increase with ageing times ;
   We chill and stiffen till we fall asleep.
Ways that were wreathed with blossom wind in thorns
Till death o'ertakes us on the silver horns.

4

Bounded, aye bounded by the fateful three,
   The weird three beldames of our mortal state,
We still are subjects of uncertainty.
   Our nearing obsequies we celebrate ;
Shrink from the sunbeam, cower before the blast,
Till length, breadth, height for mortal aid are past.

5

Yet "thoughts that wander through eternity"
    Should hold swift wings in us to aid the rise.
Forces that but exhaust should multiply,
    Renewed in nervous power that never dies;
And joys, their organs that by use efface,
Transform them fitly for the deathless race.

6

Two gravitations in the world persist,
    This to the center, that one to the sphere.
Man has the loftier gravitation missed;
    Both were his guerdon did the Word appear.
The two when rightly found are twain-in-one:
Their roundings open from and to the sun.

7

A law exists that mortals do not know,
    Whereby two currents, moving equably
And side by side in the same river flow,
    May lead the waters from or to the sea.
The valley springs, when Wisdom comes to guide,
May flow as brooks that climb the mountain side.

8

Loosen the reflex might in gravitation.
    Then, held obedient in the Master's hand,
Swift powers, that hold the planets in their station,
    Will serve for motive force by sea and land.
Wed science into God the Word, and then
All heavens and earths will meet for mights in men.

9

" Make nature plastic " ; this is the command :
  Loosen the vigor where it numbs and hides.
Evolve the scheme the Sovereign Artist planned.
  Abide in Truth for powers that truth provides.
Find Helios-Christus ; bid your hearts go still,
Nerved and responsive to the Word, our will.

XIII.

1

Science is turning slowly to retrace
  The stream that burst from eden's wounded side.
Wallace owns truths that Darwin did not face,
  And Huxley laws that Spencer dare not bide.
He who smites Word Incarnate as a stone
Upon that rock is broken bone by bone.

2

No scientist of modern time has wrought
  Unwitting loss like that one ; he has led
Learned multitudes to subterfuge of thought ;
  Fed them with dust, denied the living bread ;
Clerkly in robes pontifical has trod,
Intoning scriptures of the anti-god.

3

Needs must it be that time should breed offenses ;
  But woe to those by whom offense uprears,
Who outrage the regenerative senses
  And steep the mind in ruins, faints and fears.
The thinking ego, to dead thirdness grown,
In nature thinks the throughness to disown.

4

Such hands have decked the glittering golden bed,
 Blazoned with seeming wisdom and renown,
Where to the pleasurable fiction wed
 The cultured egoists in ease lie down,
Lost to the Word-light and its life supreme,
Lost in the evolution of a dream.

5

The culture by whose outgrowth God recedes
 From apprehensive sense is but a cheat.
Still 'tis the Spirit in mankind who pleads,
 Yet pleads no more when men with fiction meet,
And woo her, and embrace her, and instill
Her essences and with her body fill.

6

O, thou whose lips the Living Christ have kissed,
 Pure priest John Pulsford,—dear and honored name,—
Than Spencer thou art wiser scientist;
 The Holy Ghost breathes in thee for a flame,
And lo! the fiery tongues have touched thy brow;
The quickening splendors through thy speech avow.

XIV.

1

Mankind tends not to social unity;
 Not here the people's paradise is found.
The bases of divine community
 Are as a land beneath the deluge drowned.
Those who for throughness with each other dwell
Live but as tenants of the diving bell.

2

So " Looking Backward " is the scholar's dream,
   Like Campanella's " City of the Sun."
The vultures of the press exultant scream
   O'er ruined nests of social doves undone.
A fading mist of honors not to be
Proves Mexico's feigned eden by the sea.

3

All progress in the third dimension tends
   To dissolution ; Spencer saw it well.
All creatures who hold thirdness for their ends
   The substance of life's energy expel.
All men, all worlds, from fourthness that recoil,
Abide in death ; for death to death they toil.

4

The third dimension shapes an alphabet,
   Wherefrom the language of the fourth is woven ;
A stone, for carving of the statue set ;
   A shell, that for the germ's young growth is cloven ;
Dust, that for impregnation vainly plies,
Till God shall breathe through it and heaven arise.

5

The fourth is fashioned in reality ;
   The wakeful substance of all glorious dreams,
It floats, a deathless ideality,
   O'er nature's realm, and through its shadow gleams.
Substance and seeming touch ; their lines are met ;
Substance in seeming must its form beget.

XV.

1

If e'er the fourth dimensioned man should stand
  Rounding the surface, cultured and equipped,
All would be plastic to his vibrant hand :
  With justice hearted and with mercy lipped,
His path would open swift and sure and clean
By Worded force, owned as "the Nazarene."

2

George Fox divined the truth in non-resistance.
  Fight not by methods that the third affords ;
Feel to the force held in the Word's persistence.
  One man is mightier than unnumbered swords :
If through his frame arch-stellar ether flows
The world must yield, though all the world oppose.

3

See how the Lady Moon is stooping now,
  Vailing in human cloud Her argent breast.
Feel to Her presence by the lifted brow,
  The bosom of impatience dispossest.
God-time is still-time ; to the silence feel ;
It holds for Truth a form of living steel.

4

Withdraw into the stillness, till the motion
  Of God in throughness tunes the mind aright.
Lifting to ardors of serene devotion,
  The soul is energized by God in sight.
Hold to the silence, so that Judgment glides
To permeate the sense by flowing tides.

5

So find the sabbath of the Lord thy God,
   The silence of the ages and their end.
So hold through silence for a judgment rod,
   Meeting the foemen where they most offend.
All roads of last advance to Judgment run ;
Go clad with silence till the end is won.

6

In the solemnities with Peace abide,
   Peace, the white harbinger who folds the pall,
Vailing the planet, while the winds divide
   From azure air and voices fail and fall.
Solemn and still and peaceful be our tread,
Hearts to the heart of God in mercy wed.

7

See how huge unbeliefs mankind obsess,
   Soulless and shrineless, whilst the virgin Faith,
Whose lips are pressed to God for holiness,
   Is counted as a void and wandering wraith.
See, and while Faith to God thy sense attunes,
Lead faith to throughness ere the planet swoons.

8

Faith is pavilioned in eternity ;
   There she inhabits God, her deathless prime.
The fourth dimension shapes her liberty ;
   Thence rounds she to illuminate in time.
All virtues are for stars in her right hand,
And miracle is wrought her blossomed wand.

9

Enter Religion as a secret door,
    And in Religion shrine thy vital prayers.
So to Religion yield thy all for store,
    And for Religion bear thy constant cares.
For thy old self, abolished and o'erthrown,
Put on Religion's throughness, made thine own.

XVI.

1

Carved are the starred and oriented cliffs
    With stately images of Truth sublime:
Wisdom has traced in glowing hieroglyphs
    Her scriptures of the grand pre-mortal time.
By throughness thought may open to behold,
Reading the past whence futures are foretold.

2

In simple Piety, through time who keeps
    A noiseless, humble and sequestered way,
An influence presses from those upper deeps;
    Opens, enlarges, quickens, as the day
That glows through lowly corn-blades where they spring,
Pregnant with gold grain for the harvesting.

3

Sweet Piety, in purity who bides,
    Holding heart, sense, imagination clean,
Is blest and nurtured by arch-stellar tides,
    Borne in the throughness of the Nazarene.
The highest heaven, by ways no mortals ken,
Touches to serve the lowliest of men.

4

'Tis here the fourth dimension holds in store
    Faith's mightiest miracle; through these may pass
Powers that the ancient heavens to birth upbore;
    God as clear light in many-colored glass;
Transfiguration led through soul to sense;
Man radiant in the Word's magnificence.

5

Under time's wintry crust such summer sleeps
    As God for lowly meekness holds in trust.
The fiery flood, mortality that steeps,
    Weaves immortality through human dust.
She for the lilies' bloom who erst revealed
In deathless blossom wreathes Her savior-field.

6

A quickening spirit in the verse is led.
    Souls in pure piety who feel the strains,
Though stretched by age on time's procrustean bed,
    May find by faith a music in the veins.
As the vibrations through the senses chord
Their flesh will quicken, it has touched the Lord.

XVII

1

The Suffering Master spake, "sleep on, sleep well,"
    When those who should have watched for Him had slept.
Such words through ages bear a burial knell.
    Woe to the city where no watch is kept,
The city Man; safety impinges still
Upon the continuity of will.

2

The tides will ebb that bore him to success;
   Against the torrent he must swim or row.
The seas will rise his foothold to possess;
   He must build up to meet the overflow.
Trust not in God to lift thee o'er the waves,
Only as He through thine own courage saves.

3

Great men, great ages, fail by drowsiness.
   Ne'er must he slumber, though to sleep he seem,
Who would by throughness his new earth possess.
   'Tis continuity of will supreme,
Held firm in God and to His purpose wed,
That leads deliverance where hope lay dead.

4

For "thoughts that wander through eternity,"
   Hold thought that clasps eternity in time.
Build firmness through thy frame's infirmity;
   Through age elaborate the vital prime.
Call not on Jupiter to lift thy wheel,
But heave till thou shalt Zeus within thee feel.

5

Build firmness into throughness, till it breeds
   Through thy full bosom, fronts to orb the brain;
Build it in righteousness until it leads
   Motion before thee as a flying train;
Hold, till its outbirth makes thy sure, swift glance
A splendor from the Infinite advance.
   3

6

Take Purpose for thy watchful bedfellow;
 Rest in her arms and rise in her embrace;
Shrine her within thy being till she go
 As Wingéd Victory before thy face.
Make purpose final, shaping to a rod
That smites earth's granite for the streams of God.

7

This is the art of the true alchemist,
 Transmuting earth's dead dross to heaven's live gold;
Distilling from the vague aerial mist
 The interstellar ethers, till they hold
And weave about thee for pure robes of flame,
To show thee forth in Him who overcame.

XVIII.

1

The revolution of the Infinite
 Is time; and space the orbing of its whirl;
And nature in a motion of delight
 Originates, and thence its realms unfurl.
If thou wouldst be true man, a godlike son,
Think thou to nature as in God begun.

2

The universe found birth in a delight,
 And from delight and to delight it grows.
Therein be thou persistent for the right,
 Till through thy throughness the delights unclose.
Be thou delightsome, sense to spirit led:
Think God's delight into thy purpose wed.

3

Serve thus the golden opportunity,
   Till God's rich opportune through time is wound,
And heaven and earth in nuptial unity
   Meet the Twain-Oneness, and delight is crowned,
And the Bride-Bridegroom, orbing here the shrine,
Make earth-life God-life, humanly divine.

4

Await, await, await! be temperate,
   Even in thought of such delight in store.
Care for thy body, as made delicate
   By each advance to the transposive door.
Think not to hasten movement by excess
Of premature nerve-action, but repress.

5

"Grieve not the spirit"; such command is kept.
   Grieve not the body by demands unwise,
For thus the fervid animates are swept
   From the vibrations of their harmonies;
And on these harmonies, led to their ends,
The re-creation of the flesh depends.

6

But think to rest in action, rest in thought,
   Rest in emotion, rest in soul and sense,
Rest in all burden bearing,—self as nought;
   A quietude made more through loves intense
And full and fruitful as the harvest noon.
Hold coolness as the calm white Judgment moon.

7

So into Judgment let the mind be spaced,
　The heart determined and the motion timed,
Till time's impatience gently is effaced,
　And the gross energy of will sublimed,
That it may open sweetly to the tide
Of the arch-stellar ether and abide.

XIX.

1

From the electric man came man of stone ;
　From man of stone the man of flesh was led.
By such descents, mysterious and unknown,
　Grew paradise, the soft primeval bed.
The weakest of the races and their last,
Our sires were offspring from the loftier past.

2

For still creations in their course declined,
　As heats decrease by distance from their flame,
Till at the end man held a shadowed mind,
　In organs frail and senses that were shame.
Decline led on in nature's three-fold mesh,
Till the fourth opened in the "Word made flesh."

3

The world, the times, mankind were out of joint ;
　Light lessened on till darkness wove a span.
He was the Point of turn, the Pivot-Point
　On whom the rounding of the race began.
Here the "True Light" its blossomed rays unfurled ;
Soft as the dawn of dawn He touched the world.

4

And still the creature in the bondage held;
   And still mankind, as death-doomed captives drest,
Groped in the notional by magic spelled,
   Nor dwelling oped for Him nor wrought a rest.
As the white dove, far flying from its mart,
He came and met the arrow in His heart.

XX.

1

God changes not, yet ever is in change,
   By aspect to His varied people seen;
Now in the near, now in the distant range,
   Now shown through tempest, now in calm serene.
God changes not, so we do not consume;
Yet God is changed to us from bud to bloom.

2

The evolution in God's revolution
   Germs, blossoms, fruits; germs, blossoms, fruits anew.
Crises that seem but fateful dissolution
   Hold the Divine, by throughness led to view.
What though a universe should fade from sight?
Still 'twould remain, transformed into delight.

3

These heavens may vanish as a flying scroll;
   These earths mature from flower to fruit and cease;
Yet God through sense may form, as through the soul,
   And natural earth to human earth release.
The flying wheels of time in Light conceal
Their motion, but the Force will not repeal.

4

So "God fulfills Himself in many ways."
　　Through the past endings the new worlds began.
He is the Ancient of eternal days,
　　Yet evermore the Youthful Woman-Man.
Formed unto us for righteousness, we dwell
Of Him in Him for Him while times dispel.

5

But of our wantness we are fullness made.
　　God, being Fullness and to throughness led,
Clothes us as lilies of the stream, arrayed
　　In light and in its loveliness dispread.
The man-seed, clad by Him with living dust,
So finds the resurrection of the just.

6

Twain revelations wed by living thought;
　　The Infinite, that for its finite weaves
Word into scripture, finely fitly wrought,
　　Substance in seeming that the sense receives.
The fourth dimension claims the third its own;
Truth is made flesh of flesh and bone of bone.

XXI.

1

An occult shapes outside, did men but know;
　　An inner nature presses to enlarge.
This nature that we meet will overgrow
　　And senses outen on to find its marge;
Eyes ope from eyes and ears from ears emband,
Heart duplicate on heart and hand on hand.

2

This outness on man's outnesses will form
   From throughness of his innesses that weave;
Breath double for the doubled lungs, the warm
   Sweet ethers that by truth in joy receive.
Growth is arrested in the three-fold lines;
Man in the sense of observation pines.

3

Man is the slave of his impediments;
   The psyche sacrificed within its shell;
Organs, that should be four-fold implements
   Of thought and feeling, held in swoon and spell.
'Tis as if man, from single-footed spine,
Felt the bound complemental limb repine.

4

Man thinks to death as for a free escape;—
   Outward through inness should his will revolve.
God calls to outwardness: let chasms gape,
   To overbridge should be his last resolve.
We must find God in nature, large and small.
God outens to be made the All in all.

5

Nature and man are both in struggle now:
   Nature in man and man in nature nerves,
Till the full throughness shall through both avow,
   And doubled man in doubled nature serves;
More valid than the ancient grecian dream,
Divine olympus o'er his vision gleam.

6

"The expectation of the creature waits"
  Upon the manifest immortal men,
To whom arch-stellar ether opes its gates.
  For death translation waiteth here and then.
This is the earliest, latest Christian creed,
Heaven formed in earth for men as deaths recede.

7

Nature grows tenantless of psychic lives ;
  The nymph and dryad vanished long ago ;
The fay, where yet his gentle race survives,
  Lingers in hidden haunts that men forego.
A larvous world, bred from man's ills unclean,
Infests the landscape, wrought in the obscene.

8

Man is the slayer ; he depopulates
  The planet in his fierce pursuit of game.
Where'er he moves or dwells he desolates ;
  His presence breeds a base magnetic flame.
He generates the poison, swift or slow,
Where the larves hide and generate and grow.

9

So in the venomed sweat and deadly spume
  Base minds grow pregnant, and the city's dust
Is made a shadowy, sepulchral womb,
  Wherein the death-seed fashion from his lust.
From nature's wounds in ceaseless torrents ply
The spoilers of his flesh, the bacilli.

XXII.

1

"Awake, arise, my Love; the Spring has come :
   Summer her breasts of bounty will not vail.
White doves shall coo where throbbed the murderous drum,
   And for the war-call chant the nightingale.
Awake, arise, my Love, and come away";—
The Bridegroom's voice :— we hear as lovers may.

2

Nature and God, to man they both inure;
   Nature for seeming, God for substance makes ;
But man must hold the substance to endure.
   Seeming, a bubble, glistens, orbs and breaks.
Yet substance that, through seeming, forms and plies
Weaves man's new likeness lovely in God's eyes.

3

When thought is rising, as the billows roll
   In bosomed undulations of the sea,
Hold thyself o'er it in a calm control,
   Like sun-lit heaven in pure tranquillity ;
Then lead thy truths to heaven by steep on steep,
As forms of gods ascending from the deep.

4

Lift, as the sun lifts waters to the cloud :
   The thought-sea round thy orbing space expands,
But over it Intelligence is bowed
   To rule the waters and to loose their bands.
Yea, in the fourth dimension Truth to thee
May lead the human people of the sea.

5

The immortality that Christus taught,
　　Divinely natural, when grown complete,
With full redemption for mankind was wrought,
　　Man's fleshness made its theater and seat.
Its inner march the seer of Stockholm shows;
Its outer end by throughness must disclose.

6

'Tis victory o'er death, till death be slain:
　　'Tis victory for life, till life shall meet
Its vast environment, led o'er the plane
　　Of its organic space with wingéd feet.
'Twas through such outer heaven,—His own, our own,—
The Word made flesh ascended to enthrone.

7

Think then, think faithly, to the splendid hours
　　When man, his fourthness through the thirdness led,
Shall climb the glorious ascension towers
　　To float transfigured where his heavens dispread,
Opening through radiant vistas, glowing floors,
Ethereal seas, to paradisal shores.

XXIII.

1

Needs must it be, when thought awakes to double
　　And in a larger throughness to expand,
That sense should be in fear and mind in trouble,
　　And airs bring burden that once gently fanned.
Vale of death's shadow, fashioned in dismay,
Through this the dread, unknown transition way.

2

To reach the Motion whereby time was wrought,
  To find the Substance whereof space is made,
We toil by nobler will in nobler thought,
  Yet penetrate where light is lost in shade,
Where respiration by its thirdness ends.—
The vail is reached; that vail, it lifts, it rends.

3

We touch the limit of free will's persistence,
  As realizable in third dimension;
Yet here God meets us by a new existence,
  Wrought from the Word in humanly extension.
The bosom opes; a warm sweet vapor lyres;
The breath of God inflows, illumes, inspires.

4

Borne into combat by the breath in birth,
  Old forces fail, then rise in nascent powers.
Farewell the sensitive delights of earth,
  Save as the life-stalk buds for heavenly flowers.
Farewell the homes that flesh and blood made sweet;
Our frames re-fashion in God's furnace heat.

5

'Tis a dread dying of man's mortal soul,
  Led for re-birth in an immortal germ,
Whilst yet the fleshly form, in fixed control
  Of fourth dimensioned will, holds sure and firm.
To this, by calm advance of powers that rise,
We haste, nor pause; who pauses falters, dies.

6

Yet the new natural soul, at first a seed
  Sown in the old effete infirmity,
Must that infirmity absorb, implead,
  Lead through its timeness timed eternity.
Years waste, a generation fades to dust,
The man's "I will" held firm in God's "thou must."

7

Here ages concentrate to mold the years:
  Time whirls, space flies; the man of anguish, led
Through toils that ope as on envenomed spears,
  Must feed on agonies as Christus fed;
Must "live the Life," must hold a secret care
For all in all who strive the life to share.

8

More than the patriot, prophet, bard or seer,
  Concentered ever to economize,
He must build road-ways as the pioneer,
  Nor any toil of any use despise;
For vital health bound in the wasting stand,
Yet move by occult skill from land to land.

XXIV.

1

The strong man of the third dimension narrows
  To rule, a chief; the weak to crouch, a slave.
The weak pipe feebly as the thieving sparrows;
  The strong cut keenly as the sharpened glaive.
So egosocialism plumes its hordes,
As flights of sparrows, hurled upon the swords.

2

Man from his wolfness changes to a lamb,
   Owning the "Lamb of God" by sinners slain.
To bless is dangerous, more safe to damn,
   Where, in the third, Power rules by arts profane.
To "turn the other cheek" when evil smites
Provokes contempt from the shrewd knave who fights.

3

That God should see His Word-Form crucified,
   Scourged, buffeted and trampled to the grave,
Is all incredible; but as allied
   To this, that He arose in might to save.
By this that resurrection proves its worth,
The third dimension lifted in the fourth.

4

• Saint Paul spake true; this is the crucial fact.
   Else were our faith, our wounds, our labors vain.
Most miserable we, in frauds compact,
   If He arose not who to save was slain.
He freed the psyche to its utmost floor,
Led heaven through earth; His body made the door.

5

To the learned greek such faith was foolishness;
   A stumbling block to gentile, as to jew.
Vague spiritism from the flesh may press,
   Denying, failing where the Word forms through.—
Outward our movement to the many-one,
Heaven's luminous orbed angels of the sun.

XXV.

1

Thousands of generations now look down
  Upon us from time's shattered pyramids:
Cycles of ages now look up and frown
  Through stony eyeballs from their coffin lids.
To breast the third dimension's battling storm,
We bear the banners, hold the fourth in form.

2

'Tis the world's crisis, pregnant all with fate:
  The hours haste, lifting silence on their wings.
The powers that desolate or consecrate
  Encompass or incompass; shadow flings
A death-cloud o'er us to envail the scene:
Judgment stoops low the orb to overlean.

3

In the deep night-time, when the specters pass,—
  Specters of mortals that go forth in sleep,—
E'en now are some who wail "alas, alas!
  Our city's gates are broken, and the steep
Of its proud vantage, where the thrones are gilt
For splendor, drips with blood our princes spilt.

4

"And many captives, who to build its mansions
  Spent their chained lives in agonies and fears,
Whose life-blood fertilized the rich expansions,
  Crying 'O Lord! how long?' through martyred years,
Are hushed to silence; but their hearts the more
Heave to an earthquake 'neath the city's floor.

5

"And see ! where we with blackened hands have blotten
  Our names from somewhat named the 'book of life,'
And thought 'no god,' since godness was forgotten,
  A silence falls through feastings that were strife.
Let us unto the rocks and mountains call,
That they may hold and shield ere ruin fall."

XXVI.

1

There comes an hour when the importunate
  And grasping ego, never satisfied,
Is conquered, and its cruel jaws, that ate
  Into the soul's new substance, are denied,
And it lies down to impotent decease :—
From structures free its molecules release.

2

Thence, caught to fourthness in the flying whirl,
  The atoms to the human posture rise ;
A radiant image, glowing boy or girl,
  Formed to the soul for its new destinies ;
A double, that reflects, repeats, obeys
The Worded man, and serves for all his ways.

3

"Peace give I you," the Holy Master said ;
  "Not as the world, to you I give My peace."
He held such unself for an outer-stead,
  Likeness in image, doubled for increase
Of power and grace in fourth dimensioned worth,
Wrought as a vital-form of heaven in earth.

4

So we, in Him who conquer, may receive;
  For the unself is in His shadow risen,
To brighten in His shining and to weave
  Swift wings for fetters that did erst imprison.
Henceforth reigns peace! let all within us chord,
For all within is union with the Lord.

5

This is nirvana by its form and fact:
  The dew-drop glides into its vital sea;
A unity of unities compact,
  Orbed in the flow of Orbed Infinity:
Led in the bright processions of the stars,
The incarnations and the avatars.

6

But so our fleshness may revive anew,
  In a regeneration from its first;
Mankind reënter by the four-fold clue,
  And stand to serve and bless to last and worst;
By a circumference the planet feel,
Soft as the dewdrop, firm as living steel.

7

Such the New Life!—Thence we are heart-fasted
  To God Twain-One by constant rites divine,
Whereof the world knows not, till earth is wed
  To heaven:—the Cross, this is our sacred sign;
By this we conquer:—when all force had failed
The Master came, breathed in us and prevailed.

PART SECOND

"When this corruptible shall have put on incorruption, and this mortal shall have put on immortality, then shall be brought to pass the saying that is written, Death is swallowed up in victory."

1 COR. XV. 54.

4

CONVERSATION IN HEAVEN.

XXVII.

1

EARTH is the world of the unfortunates.
    Judgment I saw as Fortune on Her ball:
Her countenance to heaven illuminates;
    Earthward it wears the shadow of a pall.
'Tis so Her shadow, weaving to a robe,
Electric, penetrative, folds the globe.

2

An hand She dipped into Her roseate breast
    And from it flung aloft a silver swan;
It floated to the heaven above the west,
    Then met the Californian horizon.
There the swan rested, crimsoning, made vast;
The wings were sunset, folding at the last.

3

Judgment, Her home She in the sunset makes,
    For She is Sunset and the west Her own.
Beneath Her breast profound Pacific wakes;
    The waters quicken, rounding to Her throne.
So Judgment waits the moment of incline;
So orbs a presence,—Fortune, made divine.

4

The planet lost its Fortune in the past;
   Grown mortal and unfortunate since then.
Judgment, transformed to Fortune at the last,
   Wings the divine prosperities again.
Cleave thou to Judgment and thy Fortune find:
From Her full bosom life's full gifts unbind.

5

Judgment has cleft Her winged caduceus;
   From either branchlet blooms a blossomed rod:
Her flower of grace by throughness drips to us
   Rock honey, where we journeyed sorrow-shod.
We built for Her like swallows in the cliff;
We carved its lines to shape Her hieroglyph.

6

Now the sad planet's piercing *miserere*,
   Borne to the heart of Judgment, silenced there,
Leaves a dull ache through nations, chilled and dreary
   As frore december, broken, bruised and bare.
Heartache, numbed in heart hunger, grieves to sleep:
To frozen seas the stormy passions heap.

7

So Judgment feels, the planet's heart to find,
   To hold and fill and form a silence there;
But o'er the west Her odorous breaths unbind,
   And through the sunset streams Her golden hair.
Lo, there!—aloft, while yet the mists conceal,
Waits Judgment,—Fortune, leaning on her wheel!

XXVIII.

1

The fourth dimensioned man, as timeness narrows
  And panic in the Commonwealth anears,
Feels the advance ; 'tis as if living arrows
  By throughness pierced the earthly atmospheres ;
While the swift darts, illumined as they pass,
Burn as clear sunbeams borne through tinted glass.

2

Man is inwound, encompassed by vibration ;
  In time and tone he labors, thinks and feels,
The motion of the Word his habitation.
  Judgment is turning by Her wheel in wheels :
Fortune, aggressive, mailed in breathing balm,
Uplifts the spear, the lily and the palm.

3

Her occult wave, ethereal yet oceanic,
  Swims through all avenues of trade and strife ;
'Tis realized first as industrial panic,
  A causeless tremor of the public life.
More, more ! man's molecules are set a-flow :
The breathful doom-trump circles Jericho.

4

Such quivering, through the molecules led on,
  Precedes the march of the celestial host.
That sign in western heaven, the crimson swan,
  Heralds advance through continent from coast.
Judgment is heavened to breath of breast and brow :
Judgment, when earthened, will by this avow.

5

Men lean upon each other, in surprise
    That panic should o'er-ride where wealth abode.
Men hold to men for strength to energize,
    Feeling the mutual safeties overflowed.
The sense of common peril thrills the mart,
Where they to spoil each other strove apart.

6

Judgment is fourth dimensioned, is celestial.
    Behold Her in such glorious biding place :
Her motion rules there,—not in our terrestrial.
    Heaven sleeps, wakes, rests in the divine embrace.
Now, as by throughness manifesting here,
Heaven meets the Earth to weave one common sphere.

7

See now! the Judgment moon is disappearing,
    Mid clouds of eve in fading colors drest.
The atmosphere we meet is rising, nearing
    The sovereign ether, folding on to rest.
Now lift the bosom, fill for life's increase :
We shall breathe heaven from Judgment's lips of peace.

XXIX.

1

'Tis written in a prehistoric book,
    Whereof a symbol to us is unsealed,
" When I as O-I shall through o-i look,
    World-I as O-I shall in ✠ sun-shield."
I trace this cryptograph upon the page ;
The book may open for a coming age.

2

God shapes in man a moving vehicle,
  To bear Him through the thought-ways of mankind.
To-day one may be here, a miracle;
  To-morrow where his heavenly life is shrined;
Now, as a golden child, his form condense,
Then rise, meridian man, to visioned sense.

3

Man by corporeal receptivity
  May hold of God to his extreme degree;
Standing so wrought in formed plasticity;
  Transposing hence in fourths from thirds to be.
The organs that imprison may enthrone,
When God adopts the plastic form His own.

4

Man may from fourths evolve to thirds again;
  His fourthness thirded, statue-like and firm;
To the last sense a worlded citizen,
  Complete in organs to the final term.
See, touch and handle him, this is the same
Who seemed to perish, but who overcame.

5

One with his brethren, simple as a child,
  Humanly genial in all his ways;
First of new men, therefore as primate styled;
  Holding his orbing round through earthly days;
All in disguise, yet never in disguise;
Time for him opes, to shape new paradise.

6

For the new vital frame is of the mind,
　　And of the fourthness, germed to fill the third.
New body, that its outwardness would find,
　　Is fashioned in the concept of the Word.
If nature's men grow forth from adam-eve,
Of Christus-Christa we our forms receive.

7

Think Christus for the Sire to flesh and bone;
　　Think that we are re-wrought through Christa's womb.
Think of such incarnation, made our own
　　To resurrection o'er the mortal doom.
Think that we, fragile creatures of the sod,
Take in, take on the human form of God.

8

Think that the miracle must in us grow
　　Through mind to sense, its generating field;
Yet be not curious to probe and know;
　　Infants know not whilst in the womb concealed.
The first revealment, fitly to be styled,
Is when man finds himself a little child:

9

A wise child, such as holy angels are,
　　Conscious of breathing in the Mother-Sire;
Conscious of touching, inly from afar,
　　To God, the Fount and Fullness of desire.
Formed in unself to feeling, thought and aim;
Living alone by Christus-Christa's flame.

10

Into such state of blissful innocence
  The flood of transubstantiation flows ;
Childlike humility its evidence,
  And perfect faith and sweetness its repose.
Then, if the crystal truths within us gleam,
They are as gems that sparkle in the stream.

11

In God made flesh so let our flesh respire,
  Till transformation rounds its perfect play,
And Helios-Christus through arch-solar fire
  Is felt in Helia-Christa day by day ;
While nature, realized as seeming, wears
A tremulous live glory that is Theirs.

XXX.

1

The lungs of all mere egoistic men
  Conspire against the children of God's breath :
The organized brute passions of the den
  Combine to slay the seed of Nazareth.
Our breathings flow more free in hours of light,
But murder and disaster haunt the night.

2

The rise is that of Ixion on the wheel,
  The round as the descent of Ixion.
Slowly one climbs, by gathering mights to feel,
  Then slowly sinks the nightly round upon ;
Thence forces upward, battling all the way,
Against the world-storm that awakes with day.

3

This is a spectacle in occult space
   Unknown, unheard in history before;
A man whose motion turns against the race,
   Grasping the power, from earth that passed of yore.
He breasts the ruin, hurled the sense to fill,
From time's surcharged heredities of ill.

4

I saw a man, a Swedenborgian chief;
   He swung, suspended in an easy chair,
O'er the swoll'n cataract of human grief,
   Asleep, clairvoyant, seeking to declare;
Then, looking down to the abysmal whirl,
Espied One battling where the surges curl.

5

A spark of human pity lit his eyes;
   He cried, "throw bladders to him lest he drown";
Then shuddered and began to terrorize,
   Hiding his face within a priestly gown.
One spake, "ascend; see you, the easy chair
Sinks; 'tis suspended by a single hair."

6

Now fears o'ercame him, grew to a collapse.
   Pity was given; drawn shoreward he arose;
Then, on the sward, exclaimed, "perhaps, perhaps,
   His fiend drew that man downward by the toes;
Whilst I, his angel, putting forth a thumb,
Held him from doom by equilibrium."

7

A bird of morning nigh awoke to crow;
    He named it "correspondence; Peter's cock";
Nursed tenderly a swoll'n discolored toe,
    Crying "'tis here I met that devil's shock";
Then sniffed a scroll he held, for perfumed smells,
To "antidote the poison of the hells."

8

But one like Peter made to overlean,
    And gravely answered, "hear the morn bird's call.
The Man who struggles is the Nazarene,
    Turning His wheel 'gainst the abysmal wall.
His the uplifting force, the single hair,
That drew you shoreward in the easy chair."

9

"Alas, poor Yorick!. where the quips and cranks
    That used to set the table in a roar"?
Pure wit, wise humor, on the blossomed banks
    Of paradise, serve Truth for evermore.
The humor of the situation tells
'Gainst the false learning that the fact misspells.

10

Humor exists in God :—be humorous,
    Merry and sportive; such the lesson, meant
For all who, in the mortal fret and fuss,
    Hold heartily to serve the Word's intent.
Full oft full Truth, pursuing for the best,
Pierces offence by arrow-points of jest.

11

The Holy City, howsoever spacious,
　　John the divine was quickened to espy,
Can have no place therein for the mendacious,
　　For those who fashion and who serve a lie.
Pure truth, full truth, by varied colors shown
As emerald, ruby, sapphire, forms the stone.

12

"They jest at scars who never felt a wound";
　　They jest at wounds who can efface the scar.
That man who holds the One-Twain Word his ground
　　Owns healing where society is war.
Plumes the white dove upon the hurricane,
Breasting such wrath its home, heaven's heart, to gain.

13

He beams as if he never knew a care,
　　Yet cares for men consume his days and nights.
In the New Life we learn to hold and bear,
　　Vailing a breast that breeds and broods delights.
We conquer sorrows, that the world o'erwhelm,
As those who in the tempest rule the helm.

XXXI.

1

The eyes of man are in his purposes;
　　In fourthness we behold as we should see.
Saved from the optical uncertainties,
　　We move at ease, from accident full free.
Hence holy scripture of the just averred,
That "all his steps are ordered of the Lord."

2

The roving habitudes no more exist.
    "Just men made perfect" are as doves in flight:
They for the purpose of the way persist,
    Since God is ever made the point of sight.
In seeing God the visual sense discerns
The pathway of the round and the returns.

3

Some query, "did you meet with so and so,
    Outward or inward? tell us of their news."
We hint not what is seen, nor where we go,
    Yet never by a churlishness refuse.
On sight and speech the sacred shadows fall,
Save for a purpose that holds God in all.

4

Sufficient for the day the toil thereof:
    Sufficient for the service is the day.
The "tangled net" of seemings "blindly wove"
    We ravel not, save as it bars the way.
In the cool waters where we make our stand
The flowing Truth holds wells on either hand.

5

Pure wisdom's way is not to right nor left,
    Seeing no cause to vary or digress.
Straightforward! 'tis for this the rocks are cleft;
    Thus far, no farther but as ends confess.
Clear Truth, that couches the dense, clouded sight,
Makes mind its eye-ball for the living light.

6

To serve the great as if it were the small :
   To serve the small as if it were the great ;
To be in each the servant of the all ;
   To move as lightning, or to stand and wait :
To hold each point just as the ends require,—
Such grows to habit from the fixed desire.

7

The martinet, in stark stiff rigidness,
   Is custom's manikin, a blind machine ;
The pious ego, numbed to frigidness,
   But a dry shell, masked in a wintry screen ;
'Tis pageant, pretence, mimicry, so thin
That all may see who glance beneath the skin.

8

Nature through fictionists great fiction spins ;
   Nature through ego masses egoism ;
From her dark cabinet the "psyche" wins
   Ghostly illusions for his magic prism.
Fool-time for senile age must last avow,
Sign of the Coming, it is fool-time now.

9

Earth bows in worship to the "sacred ass,"
   The donkey ego, land to land that brays ;
Sees its own image through illusion pass,
   And makes the world its temple of self-praise.
Old Superstition felt to heavens and hells ;
New Fantasy in spectral vacuum dwells.

10

But so the end is vacancy: the void
  Rounds, doubles to without from the within :
Ego in crass, crude selfness, self-deployed,
  Shows as mere surface, proud inflated skin.
Hence the result, moving through ages on,
Is silence, vanishing, oblivion.

XXXII.

1

Sweet is the Loneliness with God that dwells,
  And, in a calm seclusion, gently keeps
Its faith, amid the partings and farewells,
  When hope goes clad in autumn's robe and heaps
The graves that hold the hours with precious dust.
God is the tabernacle of our trust.

2

Sweet are the hours, when Resignation bows
  Beside us with the God-book on her knee:
Then folds within our being, so to house
  Our sadness in her sweet sobriety.
Resigned to every change that may befall,
'Tis this extracts the sting, unweaves the pall.

3

"Lover and friend Thou hast put far from me :
  I am acquaint with darkness" of life's woe.
I enter the last time's vacuity ;
  Still, though in vacancy, content to go.
Am I in shadow, chill, funereal, vast?
"God makes the dark His covering," at the last.

4

The gold sand, sifting from time's crystal glass,
　　Spins into shadow, caught in death's dim hand.
Vision is lost as if it never was ;
　　"In the sixth hour a darkness filled the land,
And many saints who slept in dust arose " :
This may befall us in the coming close.

5

" He put away the hyssop and the gall,"
　　Holding full consciousness.   I will abide
The hour, nor shall the opiates enthrall,
　　Though lethe mingle with the airy tide.
Though God forsake in seeming, as He will
In the time's ending, hold, thou heart, be still.

6

That " God forsake," I know its meaning soon :
　　'Tis but the change of attitude : toils change ;
God changes with them, as the waning moon
　　Glides through eclipse, o'er orient heights to range,
Till her new crescent greets the morning star ;
Reborn through vanishing to avatar.

XXXIII.

1

Where are the scriptures and the hierographs ?
　　They show but as dim tracings on the wall
Of failing consciousness ; unreason laughs,
　　To see the God-prints fading, one and all.
The lights, that served for time's historic way,
Melt to a vaporous haze in mild decay.

2

The ego's mind, grasping to things unseen,
　　Projects its own illusion o'er the marge,
Reflects its thought upon the magic screen,
　　Then thinks a "spirit-world," its own discharge;
Its natural law but doubled to a scheme
Of reflex time, a dream led through a dream.

3

Ego is in the flurry ere it drown,
　　Gasping up bubbles through the watery glare:
The flame of its intelligence dies down
　　To broken hues of glamour in the air.
Ego in fantasy its content yields,
As dying Falstaff "babbled of green fields."

4

Ego dies as the fool dies, as the brute;
　　Having no Word-sense, so it hath no care;
'Tis dissolution of the dissolute,
　　The snarer dazed in pitfalls of the snare.
The spectacle expires to close the play;
The breath of Judgment blows its cloud away.

5

By night the living ethers are astir
　　To lead a languorous, dreamy, easeful swoon,
That ego feels in its self-sepulcher,
　　Greeting the flowings for a breathing boon:
They touch the lips for sweetness, they exhale
As odors of the vintage ere they fail.

6

The goblet of the air, for such libations,
    Fills with the wine of God, ethereal wine ;
But ego, led to doom by delirations,
    Quaffs it, in heart denying the divine.
'Tis bread in wine, transubstantiated clean,
Substance in essence of the Nazarene.

7

So Judgment lifts the urn for sacrament.
    See how Her cup has grown, the holy grail ;
It holds the interstellar floods unspent ;
    Ethereal seas flow from it to prevail.
"Henceforth with you I taste no cup again,
Until the Father's kingdom comes to men."

XXXIV.

1

The sons of craft, of usury and trade,
    In the great city hold their splendid feast.
'Tis here my silent solitude is made,
    A man unnoted, or esteemed the least ;
Yet here, while millions toil in sorrows clad,
I find the grail, serve as Sir Galahad.

2

The Latin Church is pageant, symbolism,
    Yet weaves a truth as Hellas did of yore.
The fourth dimension shines to touch its prism ;
    Christ, to fill all things, may its worths restore.
In hours when first his papacy began,
I met kind Leo in the vatican.

3

One, as a fellow servant, touched his bosom,
    That oped a little for such sacred spell ;
Then the White Lady from Her rod in blossom
    Shed incense there, for lo ! he loves Her well ;
Loves Her in symbol as celestial queen,
Feeling, not knowing, what the symbols mean.

4

Thence in his secret crypt he knelt adoring,
    Awed as by presence of the Paraclete,
And rose, new vigors through his bosom pouring,
    Serving in thought at the White Lady's feet.
The poor, Her poor, he loves them as his own ;
Loves them in spirit, loves to flesh and bone.

5

He grasps a socialism made divine,
    Grandly though in a mantle of disguise ;
He would undo the pact of Constantine,
    And shape Christ's church for people's paradise.
He would have prelate, king and kaiser all
Servants of God, the great to lift the small.

6

He seeks to re-instate the latin mythe,
    As Julian to save Olympus fought ;
Would raise from dust Democracy, alive
    As Lazarus, with manly vigor fraught,
To serve with Christ at table, at His feet,
Feeding the brethren where they sit at meat.

7

"Let there be justice done though heaven should fall" : •
　Let there be judgment won and earth must rise.
Judgment, impartial, generous, will disthrall
　Saints from their fantasy : God's hand supplies
The magnet that shall draw from land to land,
Till all are knit in one fraternal band.

8

Hold Leo for an object lesson thus,
　To show the old in turn toward the new.
We are "God's heretics"; he kin to us,
　Beloved of Adonai and the few
Whose lips are pressed to the White Lady's vail,
Known as the "Brethren of the Holy Grail."

———————

XXXV.

1

The interstellar ether rounds in systems
　Of realms, capacious, exquisite, twain-one,
Held in the Solar Word's divine persistence,
　The circumsphere orbed on from sun to sun.
'Tis fourth dimensional, outwound, inwound,
To shrine the belted planets in its round.

2

One God, one life, one law, one ordered scheme
　Divinely natural, its all is shown ;
Nature of nature, positive, supreme,
　Infiniverse in universe ; 'tis known
As "Theosocia," in godness shrined ;
Home of God-Man in universed mankind. •

3

- The Infinite, in timeless revolution,
    Is there for times and seasons, orbs and spheres.
From inmost outmosted for evolution,
    In all, through all, the God One-Twain endears,
Inspires, illuminates, intones, imparts;—
Man, motived into all through hearts in hearts.

4

Conceive of this by a simplicity,
    A truth-point led into the reasoning sense.
In fourth dimensioned wisdom rise and see;
    Put on a thoughtness from Omniscience;
Exalt the Word-breath till it rules the frame,
Then feel the universal by its flame.

5

So, as the Word-ways open in the brain,
    This realm a fourth dimensioned space is found.
If the ways open not, 'tis the profane
    In ego and its lusts that bars the round.
To-day the men of Jupiter and Mars
Might touch the sense, but that earth's ill debars.

6

When open earth shall touch the open sky
    And open sky with open earth achord,
The lustful ego in its wrath must die;
    As failed the tempest when it met the Lord,
And the coiled whirlpools folded to a glee,
And there was breathful rest on Galilee.

XXXVI.

1

Learned ego, "psychic," thinks o'er earth's frontiers,
   To fancy there a reflex natural law.
The "medium" spiritist reveals the "spheres";
   The same old world, blown by a windy flaw,
Through death's dim outlet, to a second state;
A "summer land" where pastimes never sate.

2

'Tis natured thought, in third dimension yet;
   The funeral banquet hashed for birth-time feast;
A spectral show in lavish splendor set,
   To a perpetual festival released;
The tree of old self-wisdom fruited rife,
The coiled snake hissing, "this the tree of life."

3

Ego thinks ether as fluidity;
   A superserviceable fund of force;
A fierier flowing of the nature sea,
   Waiting his summons for the onward course;
To waft his chariots through lucid air;
To glorify the feast and charm him there;

4

Perchance to lengthen on the span of years;
   To renovate for age its dry remains;
Arrest the planet's crisis that anears;
   Lead fresh fertility o'er wasted plains;
Enarm the sciences with magic might,
And spin the planet in his self-delight.

5

Ego has reaped the globe ; its barns are full,
    And now he whets the scythe for larger swing ;
Has roused the doom-storm, and its wrath would lull ;
    For safeties thus the "second sphere" would bring.
Ego, like conquering Alexander, sighs
New worlds to ravish ; in his dream he dies.

6

I saw a ghost ; he lived for self-applause
    And in a dream of battles bowed the head.
Bound by the dread, inexorable laws,
    He haunts the plains that reddened for his tread.
As the "red specter," dripping through and through
With sanguine stains, he wails o'er Waterloo.

7

He was a psychic too ; a star, "his star,"
    Fixed in imagination, lured him on.
Europe was chained to his triumphal car,
    And the wild war-fiends crowned Napoleon.
There's an astrology that coils in fate ;
A star that falls, a mill-stone for its weight,

8

And by its fall it crushes. Howsoe'er
    The man who serves the star may rule and rise,
His feet are fast within the evil snare ;
    He haunts the wrecks of his dead empiries ;
For all the wrong he wrought, the blood he spilt,
Flames wreathe, his heart shows but the dagger's hilt.

XXXVII.

1

We who are of the Nazarene creation,
   Mortals conserved to immortality,
Own the Divine in natural operation,
   So daily quickening as we daily die.
We touch men outly by the four-fold feel;
Truth dwells in us, in effort to reveal.

2

Nature's revealment, by its lines, is writ
   In the three kingdoms that from time began.
The Nazarene revealment, subtly fit,
   Thence re-creates creation into man.
Word-man in man, the God Twain-One lifts free;
Brahm in the lotos of the human sea.

3

Judgment, when full, is opening, is emergence.
   The Word that grew in flesh, the term fulfilled,
Lifts, by an infinite proceeding urgence,
   The twain-one life, where nature pierced and killed.
Christ, the God Bridegroom, to the nuptials glides,
And all his own arise as bridegroom-brides.

4

See how the symbols open into fact;
   How the obscure shines in the God-light clear.
Man, scriptured in the Nazarenian pact,
   Finds the full re-creation fashioned here.
All things are wrought as prophecies foretold;
The Woman's kingdom breasts, mankind to fold.

5

Christ leads forth Christa, whom mankind's offense
  Rejected, held from manifested sight.
Folding the Woman's Word from sense to sense,
  She orbs humanity in Love's delight.
Hence avatar; the Nazarenian reign;
One-twain humanity in God One-Twain.

6

Old scripture grew from fourth, but vailed in third,
  Vailed in the partial; therefore "known in part."
New scripture, flowing in the Bridal Word,
  Leads the completeness on through heart to heart.
Henceforth no possibility of fall;
The heart-united race; God all in all.

7

See how the Infinite is leading through
  The finites, touching even to a verse;
Sprinkling, by fervid airs, Life's honey-dew,
  For resurrection o'er the planet's hearse.
Let us abide in hope, in God full strong,
Thrilled by glad preludes of the Lord's new song.

XXXVIII.

1

The attitude of time is drifting, drifting.
  Now Peoples in calamity array,
While secretly moves on the final sifting.
  Souls feel the treacherous ooze through nature's play:
Stupidity encroaches on the sense:
Oppressive ego turns on the defense.

2

Where, heretofore, we dwelt in worldly angers,
  Pressing as combatants on hostile spears,
To-day we toil grasped in a belt of languors;
  Hot were the enmities, now chill the fears.
Men, while they crowd each other to the wall,
Quiver as forest leaves about to fall.

3

The airs are dense with palpable oppression;
  A yellow vapor clouds the jaundiced skin:
Life ebbs away in languid, slow repression;
  Death too is languid, death and pain and sin.
The winding streams of thought and feeling, slow,
Wearied and darkling, on to Lethe flow.

4

The zest of vice is palling in the vicious;
  Ego, the snake, embeds his coil in slime;
The impiously gay, the meretricious,
  Feel in self-motion that is losing rhyme.
Judgment, exacting to the final coin,
Confronts mankind to penetrate the groin.

5

Of old, men thought to sex by upward lift,
  But now approach it by the downward tread.
God-life and sex-life are in fatal rift;
  Chasm twixt heaven and nature's procreant bed.
Here the last profanation of the race;
Here the coiled dragon in Life's holy place.

6

Here 'tis that Judgment touches to unseal.
   The Awful Woman who is robed in doom
Pierces the sexual sense, the feel of feel,
   To quench the fever-blaze that fed the tomb.
'Tis here at last that Judgment lifts Her vail.—
Hail, Helia-Christa! so shalt Thou prevail.

—

XXXIX.

1

Men strive to ward off doom by devious arts;
   To battle God the Twain-One by a jest;
Blaspheme the gospel of the counterparts;
   War by the dragon's flaming coil and crest.
Sex-falsehood in sex-evil, mightening still,
Defies the Judgment, dares the Woman's will.

2

In the dim night I crossed the sex frontiers,
   Led in the motion of the Nazarene.
Ego has champions, ghostly cavaliers,
   Myriads in one, the common libertine;
Massed to a common purpose, common lust,
For war against the Woman's Word they thrust.

3

God-sex or ego-sex, such is the issue;
   All causes merge into the final cause.
Ego would penetrate the gauzy tissue
   Of the new flesh: the sexual vortex draws
Its myriads to weave a common whirl.—
Judgment now enters as a Fair Young Girl.

4

The Protestant denies the Word in sex;
  The grim agnostic follows in his train;
The Romanist strews time with marriage wrecks,
  Taking the nuptial name of God in vain.
Creedless men-apes and zealots of the creed
Are one, to serve sex-ego in its need.

5

All sexual crimes are one by last resort,
  And with all ills to common ends unite.
All criminals hive in the common "scort,"
  And by its lust-fire nerve their venomed might.
Here the dehumanizing powers agree,
Chaining mankind in common anarchy.

6

But Judgment enters anarchy. How still,
  Sweet and yet awful is that Woman Grace!
The chalice that She lifts, no drop to spill,
  Holds life or lethe, led to all the race.
Her feet are on the whirlpool, and the rain
Of odors from Her bosom falls amain.

XL.

1

Explore Chicago's Exposition grounds.
  For this the lavish millions were bespent.
A pallid ring the multitude surrounds,
  On spoilage, luxury or learning bent.
The vapor-cloud of Judgment, white and thin,
Weaves o'er the hair, it gathers on the skin.

2

The chirping crickets fail before the frost,
  Whose pallor in the air weaves pestilence :
So the sex-insects, myriads, are crost
  Through all their pastime by a chilling sense,
Which, to the lusts of life within their hold.
Instills the feeling, that the last is told :

3

That autumn is upon them with its blasts.
  But that eyes close in glamour, they would spy
Shade from the rising World-Soul, that o'ercasts
  The proud pavilions of their harlotry.
Mark there the shadow of the Fateful Hand,
Fingers that ply the sex-sense to disband.

4

Thousands on thousands, fairy violins,
  Lutes, trumpets, drums! the fairy song-horns blow.
Now fairyland is loosed ; the music spins
  Into a blithe refrain, "home, home we go."
The breast of the World Mother has set free
The Word-seed of the new humanity.

5

And quiet folk of Mars and Jupiter,
  From space-ways of the sun's etheric flow,
Charmed by the melody to follow Her,
  Vibrate into the World-Soul, winding so
A motion that is populous with lives ;
Fairies that swarm as bees to summer hives.

6

Be not thou by the murmurous motion vexed
   If it should wind fay-bugles in thine ear.
"Motion that breeds to song," so saith the text
   In Wisdom's book, "bespeaks the Coming near."
'Tis from the small in germ great acts proceed;
God's kingdom grows from viewless human seed.

7

The bubble city, with its bubble show,
   Whirls in a common panic of mistrust.
Guests on the golden mendicants bestow,
   Then turn aside in sorrow or disgust.
Sex-lust in lust of coin the bubble bred;
The World-Soul through it hath her shadow led.

8

Advance again, but now to Notre Dame,
   The proud cathedral lofty o'er the Seine;
See o'er it streaming heaven's broad oriflamme,
   Starred all with golden lilies: Judgment came,
And flung Her ensign free upon the breeze,
O'er the gorged city of time's harlotries.

9

Blood spatters the gay boulevards; through the stone
   Clear eyes may still glimpse where the Commune bled.
Judgment stood silent, but She heard the groan
   Of the chained People, She drew home their dead.
Yet lo! Her dead, all, all whose lives were spent
To pave Her pathway, serve the last event.

XLI.

1

Men catch at straws to battle with the storm,
  To shield them from flame-tempest and white rain :
Their futile schemes for corporate reform
  Are wattled huts against the hurricane :
They brood o'er serpents' eggs, within the bed
Of the slain dove, to hatch young snakes instead.

2

The bankrupt planet swings to liquidation :
  Let us praise God for penetrative light.
Ego has held and ruled the situation,
  Claiming inversive progress for its right ;
Doing its worst, it hastes to coin a worse.
The plague-spot festers in Life's universe.

3

I saw by night a worn old ruin fall,
  Built by inversive morals long ago.
The tremors of the Judgment touch the ball
  Of Ego's sex-force ; there's a sudden throe
Of human earthquake in the quivering soil,
As if the world-snake rounded to uncoil.

4

But, moving on, there was a stranger sight ;
  A fire like blazing oil before me ran ;
Fierce winds, that kindled ego to his might,
  Took fire to penetrate his organed van.
In every spark thereof a fairy drew
His bow, to wing a piercing arrow through.

5

Woman is ego's point of last objective ;
    'Tis by the ego that the matron breeds.
Woman, subservient, is yet protective,
    Shielding the man-snake, on her life who feeds.
Woman, her sense of sense in common rape,
Wings the destroyer for the last escape.

6

A fairy sped into my nerve of vision,
    Naked, rose-crowned, as cupid with his bow :
Never did paradise or fields elysian
    A lovelier image to the sight bestow.
His arrow sang true to a blessed aim,
A warbling melody its flight became.

7

Judgment begins in littles ; first a point,
    Small as such fire-point, in the world's huge sphere ;
Yet it has power to loosen, joint by joint,
    Man's bulky frame, till ego disappear.
Such Word-motes, arrowing the polar ice,
Dissolve time's glacier ; then blooms paradise.

XLII.

1

Judgment grows sensible, to touch the sense,
    For sense of coming throughness, all Her own :
Herein is met the dawn of evidence.
    By hues in hues, to mortals all unknown,
Sunrise and sunset through each other burn,
With colors from the God-rise in return.

2

The permanent invades the transitory,
  With lusters that from love the tints distrain ;
A glory and a glory and a glory,
  Bride, Bridegroom and the beauteous nuptial train !
When Judgment lifts to God-light on the brow,
Aurora coronalis will avow.

3

Sit with me in this cloistered nook awhile.
  Now listen ; 'tis the Light that in thee sings.
There is an archway to this hallowed pile,
  Fronting full east, named as "the door of kings."
'Tis to receive the magi of the star,
Wise men who come to hail the Avatar.

4

In such tremendous confluence of fate,
  Wings of pure flame, from shoulders and from brow,
Lift tremulous ; the body slips from weight,
  Into the weightless ether ; while the prow
Of the first music-breathing argosy
Slides into sight from heaven's ethereal sun.

5

From weight to weightlessness !—the skylark fails,
  And the empyrean eagle droops his wings.
Judgment, by weightlessness, o'er weight prevails ;
  This is a gift that full deliverance brings.
Her own, who serve the Word's imperial gate.
"Run and not weary, walk and never faint."
  6

6

Yet, ere the new born cast begins to dapple,
  The chanting stars shall hail Love's prime reborn;
And blithe fay minstrels, in their bosom chapel,
  Wake orisons for God-rise in the morn:
Then all the nerves at-one as lyre-strings play,
Attuning so for God-time in the day.

7

Soft, soft! bid Promise fold glad wings in prayer,
  "Thy kingdom come, Thy will be done below."
Change must avow by weightlessness from care;
  The bosom blest by lips from Lilimo'.
Weights of the spirit, mind and sense release
To final weightlessness: the End is peace.

8

Judgment is moving by the flowing tide:
  The Beauty of the Morning meets the lands.
Suffered not yet to touch Her balmy side,
  We feel the foot-rise through the wavering sands.
Lo! She will lift Her naiads on the crest
Of billowed life, brides for the marriage drest.

9

Poised in the conflux of twain gravitations,
  Man of full fourthness, holding in his whirl,
Rules for his round by pure equilibrations,
  Infurling here, there shaping to unfurl.
Set in the "door of kings," to serve he stands,
The flames his chariot and the winds his wands.

XLIII.

1

The troubles of the time do not abate.
　Now I am troubled in them, for the few,
The burden-bearers of such sad estate,
　Who hold in all the failures to pursue.
I saw a stork beside a marshy stream,
Where he had found his food and fed his dream.

2

One spake, "this is a man of many parts,
　Who fed on human instincts, kindly good,
And swallowed wealth by socialistic arts,
　And for a leader of the people stood :
But now he droops to failure, harping still,
' My frogs conspire to outrage me, or kill ;

3

" 'And if I am destroyed, the marsh will dry,
　And the poor creatures, whom I sought to save,
But who deny me, perish utterly.' "—
　Then rose the frog-chant, "hark the knave, the knave!
Years we have spent our flesh to fill his maw.
Let us invoke the gunners and their law."

4

"Glad tidings of great joy to all this land,"
　Spake, in his sharp, quick voice, a shining fay ;
"Stork, stork! deny the greed-itch, set your grand
　Broad wings, release the frogs and sail away."—
If one would serve the people in its toil,
He must conserve and not consume the spoil.

5

No man who claims, but will not lift the load,
   May hope deliverance in the coming life.
The chief, upon the "public ass" who rode,
   Is overthrown when judgment hours are rife.
We toil through cares to reach the end of cares ;
He 'scapes the burden who the burden shares.

6

The stork bowed to me, thus to pierce my hand
   For blood, but no more drops of blood he drew ;
Then soared forlornly to a far-off land,
   Croaking, "alas, friends fail me, life adieu!
Through toilsome years I strove that frogs might thrive ;
Now none will aid to keep my flesh alive."

7

Blame not the stork, for that he is a feeder ;
   Joy that he holds kind thoughts for such as feed.
His error is to drape himself as leader,
   With promised food-gifts to the frogs in need.
Frog marsh in "Labor Unions" oft is shown,
And "walking delegates" for storks are known.

8

Reforms decease for want of true reformers,
   Captains and Commissaries, rank and file.
The blatant demagogues, the scolds and scorners,
   By lack of honor fail, not lack of guile.
No dwellers in the marsh transform till when
Ego has flown ; marsh becomes corn-field then.

XLIV.

1

I saw a Poet who had drawn a skin
    Of egoized remembrance to a trail,
And through death's portals, but inclosed therein,
    Projected, shone as comet with its tail.
Stripping the fringe, whilst pangs rose to pursue,
The trail, like to his ghost, to face him grew.

2

Then fears o'ertook him, for himself he saw,
    Man who had lost his shadow, and the ghost,
That was his semblance, smote him with an awe,
    Being the self that he had known the most.
Hence he beheld his egoized career
Packed in a man-skin, thus to re-appear.

3

But as the wraith removed, new voice was his ;
    Yet 'twas a voice that minimized, made small
As are the notes of atomics that whiz,
    Or droning insects on the summer wall.
The strident voice of natured time had flown ;
Gone with the shade the voice that it had known.

4

Afterward hung the shadow on a limb
    Of that which seemed a tree's o'erhanging bough,
As linen from the laundry ; only dim,
    Blanched memories of ego showing now.
He to regain the vestment reached and smote,
Toiling to don it as his ancient coat.

5

Clad with the wraith, he felt himself in it
    A pallid shadow of memorial time ;
Felt as a wraith, as vapors when they flit
    Lifting in moving mist-wreaths, hence to climb
Out of the deep, dense shadows of the glen
To meet the morning light, dissolving then.

6

Through urging toils out of the coat he slipt ;
    Then One approached him, lovingly who said,
"Son, turn the garment outside in" : it whipt
    Upon him, flung him, billowed on his head,
Till from such fight anon the shadow lay
Turned inside out, a shadow lost in day.

7

Turn inself into unself ; this is how
    Manhood persists to Life's enduring prime.
Cleave the illusions to the breast and brow ;
    Strive unto clearness through the shadowed grime.
Turn outside in from the inversive state ;
Inhabit sunshine ; hold the opening gate.

8

Dumbness is better than the strident voice,
    And blindness than the egoistic sight,
And deafness than the hearing that decoys,
    And tastelessness than lawless appetite,
And smelllessness than smellness of the swine,
And sexlessness than sex made undivine.

9

In Judgment's hidden holy house 1 dwelt.
  Yet hours therein held days of mortal pain;
For there I learned the processes that melt
  The selfness, all as ice dissolved by rain.
Hence I serve now therefrom, till cold and gloom,
Transposed, reversed, show paradise in bloom.

XLV.

1

Stripping their shades, saints show ridiculous;
  Man, growing Godward sane, seems nature's fool.
The sons of ego cry, "come, tickle us.
  They who most tickle ego hold the rule.
This is the road to glory; they who spin
The ego to its dance by pastimes win."

2

So men are tickled trout, that Pretence catches,—
  Fisher, who gropes in hollows of the brook
To fill his creel: the silly ones he snatches,
  Or baits them with false pleasures for the hook.
Temptation tickles; every cunning ill
Befools the sense, a ruin to fulfill.

3

Be not thou one of nature's tickled trout;
  Barter not life's rich harvest for a straw;
Turn temptative illusion inside out;
  Hold throughness to thee for transposive law.
Pretence and ill, mankind that crush and curse,
Rule by an evolution turned inverse.

4

Would man but lead God's throughness fairly through,
　Divinely natural from soul to skin ;
Holding till organs by such potence grew
　Ripe, roseate, radiant to out from in,
He might transpose to statue, stone or star,
Changing to follow God in avatar.

5

There is an eye that might transpose the eye,
　Making it luminous to cleave the night ;
Absorbing through its organs all things nigh
　Sacred and precious for divine delight.
Ego is in the eye for mote and beam ;
Transform the vision to the sight supreme.

6

Hold thou the eye for that God wrought it for ;
　Turn by clear vision to the truths that are.
False pleasure is a falling meteor,
　But glorious Truth the goddess in her car,
The Goddess Judgment ; lest thy searchings fail,
Look thou to that of Her within the vail.

7

The pillars of the man-world shall be shaken ;
　The curtains of the woman-world rent twain ;
Falsehood in fallacy be overtaken,
　And evil in its garnishings be slain.
The heaven of I opes through the heaven of O.
Judgment, Bride-Bridegroom, leads from Lilimo'.

XLVI.

1

Mankind is waiting for the Social Word,
   Shaping the solid soil through fictioned foam.
Municipality is thus restored ;
   The race imparadised, no more to roam.
New State is waiting for New Church in birth ;
New Church in State holds Saviorhood for earth.

2

Heaven smiles upon us through the crimsoned leaf ;
   Faith, like autumnal woodlands in decline,
Arches o'er cloistered shades a blazoned wreath,
   Fanned by the pensive memories of the prime.
Faith served as Moses by the budding rod ;
Then vanished, but the burial is in God.

3

Belief survives, but as the tinted bough ;
   Leaves, colors there, whilst bloom and fruit are lost.
I saw a Man, a Laborer at the plough ;
   Four mighty steeds, red maned, before Him tossed.
All four-fold were their breathings, four-fold one ;
So Christus drave the horses of the sun.

4

The Seasons four, urged by His breathing fire,
   Trod in a proud arch-natural liberty,
Treading the air, yet trampling to the mire
   By flames : their fiery hoofs woke harmony.
The plough, for ploughshare, held a living wheel :
It pulverized the soil as flesh might feel.

5

Lo! 'tis the Ploughman Christ who ploughs the nations;
    The People's Word is fashioned to the plough:
The turning of the wheel, in swift vibrations
    Four-fold through man, His doing shall avow.
'Tis Christ in Christa cleaves the judgment ground;
Circles the planet by the seasons' round.

6

He gave a leaf; it reddened in the palm,
    Dissolved to mist, a gauzy mantle spun,
Colored as Joseph's robe, held breathing balm.—
    So clad, I find mild autumning begun;
A song of Judgment in the season's grief;
The rise of God in falling of the leaf.

7

To pleasurings have oped the sun-stained leaves,
    That twine such coronal upon my brow.
Still 'tis through pleasuring that Judgment weaves;
    Glad winds, Her messengers, are sportive now.
In the etheric auras blithesome sprites
Shape for the Word-whirl, as the song invites.

8

The fire-veined poppy droops her languid lips,
    Spent by the day's brief dalliance with the sun;
The pregnant ether, from her heart that drips,
    Diffuses drowsy death, her goal is won.
See now, the crimson poppies fail, they yield
No gifts to crown Life's gold-grained harvest field.

XLVII.

1

Broad wings, displayed to rearward and to van ;
   The body orbed to move in living wheels ;
Four lengths, where one subserved the natured man ;
   Four breadths, where one for his expanse reveals ;
Four heights, for one that serves his fall and rise ;
Thus shaped the cherub to Ezekiel's eyes.

2

Yet manhood, with such range of organs fraught,
   Into our apprehension may be led.
Man, through his fourthness to the acme wrought,
   With fifth dimensioned force is filled and fed ;
All sons of God, our "atmas," kindred still ;
Such glorious ones the Cosmic Word fulfill.

3

Old Papal Rome, subversive dominant,
   Shaped by inversions from Ezekiel's plan ;
Its pivot-point a four-fold hierophant,
   Four magi knit to seeming cherub man ;
Four giant selfs, sex-dried but sex-inled ;
Four brains in one, one body and one bed.

4

The fourth of these is perished, buried low,
   In the obscure below the deep of deep.
The real Fourthness crossed their line to show ;
   Upon their wakefulness He folds a sleep.
So, through their motion, is cessation prest,
And in their restlessness a coming rest.

5

"Enter the strong man's house to spoil his goods."
  Rome's mighty house is entered, to deliver
To births of breathing life the multitudes,
  Bound as the ice flakes in a frozen river.
A fire is borne the waters to unchain.
Judgment is opening from the Word One-Twain.

6

So Rome is moving to out-think its thought,
  To bind its bindings, to unwill its will;
That thus the symbolisms, that it caught
  In priestly magic, may unweave from ill.
The terror, that made God's free house the jail
Of chained mankind, "its gates shall not prevail."

7

For this think lovingly toward the great
  And ancient Church, the apostolic see.
Redeemed mankind shall reconstruct the gate,
  With sacred womanhood at-one to be:
Then through the doors full oft to sight may glide
Petrus with Petra, bridegroom blest in bride.

XLVIII.

1

Who knows the secret of the planet's pain?
  A Woman doth, Her name "Immensity."
She was before the sunshine or the rain,
  Yet the Sun loved Her and She was the Sea.
From nature to Her flowing robe we cling:
She moves amid mankind by mothering.

2

Who knows the secret of the planet's birth?
   A Woman doth; She bore it on Her knee.
Through shadowed soil She led aromal earth,
   The substanced essence for humanity.
She entered it to rule for day and night;
Through its small orb whirled for Her space, delight.

3

Who knows the secret of the planet's lapse?
   A Woman doth; She hungered for Her child,
Starved and a-cold; She wove etheric wraps,
   Diffusing loving dews, warm, fragrant, mild.
She led a living spirit through the sense
Of loss and shame; She being Providence.

4

Who knows the secret of the planet's age?
   A Woman doth; She bears within Her breast
The annals of the human pilgrimage.
   Race after race, drawn to Her bosom, rest
In the starred ether, with full being rife.
She is their home; She is the Blessed Life.

5

Who knows the secret of the planet's gift?
   A Woman doth; a drop of virgin dew
Conceived of God, the Word-babe to uplift;
   That Babe twain-one forth from Her Being grew,
And growing still absorbs the planet's woe;
Transforms it to delight, delivering so.

6

She whose large heart conceived the human planet,
   To Her I turn in time's dread hour of doom.
Her mercy-winds, that flow to bathe and fan it,
   Weave through my Worded thought a light in gloom,
A splendor that is blessing; heart and mind
Her infinite sure purpose there may find.

7

All worths that shape religion hold the Mother :
   Religion lives but by the Mother's gift.
Creeds, that contend and clash with one another,
   Still hold a promise, urging to the lift.
Rome holds a dominance in time's despite,
Since Rome once felt the Lady of Delight.

8

Christa is in organic Christendom ;
   Its heavens are in Her, Woman of the Sun.
The huge self-dragon sprays mankind, to numb
   Its sense, that feels to find the Twain-in-One.
The Infinite All-Mother 'tis who strives
In judgment, as warm Spring to wake the hives.

9

Frogs heap in all the chambers of the houses,
   Whilst blood is on the lintels of the doors ;
But Christa to Her heart the church espouses,
   And in Her sacrament its life restores.
Silence shall brood where now the organs peal,
Tongues fail from utterance, then Her ends reveal.

10

The fiery opal fashioned from Her mist :
   The diamond grew from Her etheric rain ;
Gold sparkled where Her solar lips had kissed,
   Through pregnant auras, thrilled to unrestrain :
Lights of Her presence flame from gem to gem,
All as one stone in Christa's diadem.

11

The roots of myth and miracle are in Her :
   Science and song in Her their germs conceive ;
Manhood uplifts by righteousness to win Her,
   And from Her womb new being to forthweave.
Christus shone first, the Alpha of our past ;
Christa unvails, Omega at the last.

XLIX.

1

Rome is the best that ever shaped to worst :
   The worst that ever cumbered o'er the best ;
Fountains of life flow in her streams accurst ;
   There the white dove, and there the dragon's crest :
Her hand is to all purses, and her ear
To the last secrets is held ever near.

2

Rome is the kindest and the cruelest ;
   Her fangs pierce hapless, blinded mortals through :
All time's hypocrisies by her are drest
   For vain illusion, and the motley crew
Of priests, who are her players, hold the kings
And peoples spell-bound by the mimickings.

3

Rome rises, as the bosomed sphinx, above
    The fierce, red desert that men call "the past."
No man the secret hath divined thereof;
    All who essayed have perished, being cast
Below the mystery, as souls, alone
Who faced Medusa, and were grooved in stone.

4

Rome is that one who names herself as "Mother."
    Matron, yet murderous, from her bosom weaned,
The toiling babes she grasps, to pierce or smother.
    Nations escape her soul-care smirched, bemeaned;
Yet nations, groping from barbaric night,
Hailed her, their savioress by love and light.

5

Rome is the witness of Illumination.
    Entombed within her lives the hidden fire;
Yet the black magic, the abomination,
    Works with the fetish, serving her desire:
So all the crafts, by craftiest worldlings known,
Fail when they meet the craft that is her own.

6

O Joy! that there is "something in her embers,"
    That through the cold of ages yet survives;
A something in her, that of heaven remembers,
    And for the coming of its kingdom strives;
A something, that would lead a shining now
From the arch-pontiff's bosom to his brow.

L.

1

Rome the magnificent, Inheritress
    Of all that imaged god or goddess, when
The Spirit, brooding o'er time's wilderness,
    Diffused religions through primeval men ;
Needs must that, in her vitals, should survive
The awesome past, a power to hold and strive.

2

The thunders of Olympus hide in her,
    And the survivals of the bolt of Jove.
She arms her missionizing crucifer
    With the old spells whereto the magi strove.
Faith, as a setting sun, orbs through her lids ;
The same old faith that reared the pyramids.

3

The blade of Cæsar in her crozier hides ;
    Staff of the shepherd for such priestly hands ;
It cleaves asunder, as no glaive divides,
    Faith from its reason, freedom from its wands.
Mark ligna-yoni, cross above her bed ;
Ligna dishonored, yoni stricken dead.

4

Rome is a curse, evolved from benediction ;
    A benediction, spell-bound in a curse ;
A violence that leads envailed affliction ;
    A whirl of selfhoods, held in bad from worse.
Rome "storms across the ages"; Israel's hordes,
Levites with war horns, Joshua with the swords.

7

5

Yet Rome led forth by priestly rites to bless us,
    Her common people held in common good ;
Then donned imperial garb, the shirt of Nessus,
    Took on the pestilence and in it stood,
Whilst, to her thought, she wore the seamless robe
That Christus gave, to fold it round the globe.

6

Steadfast to purpose, tireless, unrelenting ;
    The best and bravest of time's neophytes
With slow, sure skill, unpitying, unrepenting ;
    She trains to feed with life her ghostly rites ;
Arms them with miracle, made falsely true,
All means held lawful for her end in view.

7

Rome made sterility her continent,
    And impotence its horizon and sphere.
She holds for Christ, as in her immanent,
    But coffins Christ, vailed on her burial bier.
She weaves white robes, as matron all divine,
But folds with Circe where she herds her swine.

8

She holds an evolution, but supprest,
    And thereby bred to pestilential breath ;
Her spores invade the universal breast
    Of man and woman, for dissolvent death.
Crouched on the globe, that writhes beneath her knee,
She thunders, "heaven is closed, I hold the key."

LI.

1

Rome is a serpent, through all peoples wound,
   Whose crest uplifts o'er seas and lands to smite ;
An adder striking at the head, that ground
   Of permanence with flesh may not unite ;
Social dissolvent, claiming yet to be
Sole foundress of divine society.

2

Yet Rome is neither social nor theistic ;
   A congeries of many sects in one,
She burrows in the caverns of the mystic,
   Her face turned from, not to, the Spirit Sun.
Her good are good, in logical despite
Of the proud pivot-force that is her might.

3

A self-involving motion holds her twined,
   To spin through centuries a deathly coil.
Serpent in earth-snake, proprium of mankind,
   She generates a dense magnetic oil ;
Slips through all obstacles that interpose,
Rounding success to ruin at the close.

4

The oil gives odor ; nostrils that inhale
   Inflate, to think her ghostly superstition
The city of our God, above the pale
   Of reason reared, Saint John's majestic vision.
The oil exudes, finding a mortal vent
In pious, languid, carnal self-content.

5

Mock mass, mock marriage, mock community!
    Through all her ghostly ritual she spins
Fictitious union, real disunity
    Of man with God,—the body of the sins.
For captive sinners, gorgeous, festive, gay,
Hers the light yoke and the unburdened way.

6

Egypt, more pious, reverent, genial far,
    From earlier faith more stately ritual wrought.
Christ, as Osiris, touching by a star
    Into her consciousness, led happier thought,
And Christa, One with Him, for worth was shown
Humanly grand, as holy Isis known.

7

Buddha, from pre-incarnate Christus, drew
    The nobler charity that Rome denies;
He touched the throughness for a secret clue:
    Glimpsed to "the Path"; Rome stumbles there and lies
Gross, heavy, smirched with every wealthy ill,
Self-eased, self-amorous, self-seeking still.

8

Rome would make history her palimpsest;
    Effacing truth that sacred Wisdom scrolled,
And over-writing all with texts at best
    Misread, or plagiarized from ages old,
And miracles that spiritism weaves,
Where nature imitates and self deceives.

9

Rome is a mystery in third dimension,
   Based upon groups of unsexed magic men,
Who, age by age, scheme with a fixed intention
   To rule mankind by priestliness, as when
Brahm reigned o'er India by a sacred caste,
Or Samuel smote Philistia to devast.

LII.

1

True scriptures of the ancient days predict
   The old world's ending in a whirl of fire.
Our Mother, Judgment, never doth afflict;
   Ends flow as music from Apollo's lyre;
The Sun God, pouring through aerial seas
Floods of rich life that ope to melodies.

2

Ruins of men exhale by a cremation.
   A spicy breath of aromatic flame,
Etheric blent with psychic respiration,
   Dissolves the flesh, that sleep at first o'ercame.
The shadowings of organs trail away,
As night-mists melting on the lips of day.

3

This lyric verse is all improvisation:
   Through reasoning truth the verbal rhythm plies.
So, in the closure of this generation,
   She who is Melody shall improvise:
Christa, by sweetness of Her reasoned strain
Leads living raptures through the human pain.

4

Loosen the bands that held the tempered mesh
 Of soul-knit shadows; song is flying, flying.
The undulant, swift measures meet the flesh
 At nerve and pore; illusive life is dying.
The world that was is lost beneath the waves
Of minstrelsy, that overwhelm the graves.

5

The amphora is pierced, that held the flood
 Of solar nectar sealed from mortal lips;
Clear as celestial ichor, warm as blood
 From summered spring in paradise, it dips
Mankind into its passion, by surprise,
Faint as dreamed odors that through trance arise.

6

Now Judgment in Her melody advances,
 Slowly as mist-wreaths from ethereal streams;
Whilst all her quickenings glide on through trances,
 Born of calm sleep envailed in odorous dreams.
The strain that ends the sure, mysterious quest
Is pity, dearest, tenderest, sweetest, best.

LIII.

1

The Twain-in-One remains; all imaged gods
 And goddesses from human thought are fled.
Christus-in-Christa wreathes the judgment rods
 For Love's new marriage scepter: from the thread
Of lingering human life that held their twine,
They weave rich purples, royal robes divine.

2

Beams forth the One-in-Twain ; all lights are gone
    That, by self-reason's fantasy, were tossed,
To deck the marshes of oblivion
    With mimic lusters, and to weave the frost
Of the self-nature, waste and withering,
To frail, false hues of preternatural spring.

3

The sun robes in Their glory, and the moon :
    One-Twain, Lord-Lady, orb-in-orb appear.—
Stand with me in the Judgment rise ; 'tis noon,—
    Noon as in God-time ; centered in the sphere,
The splendor of pure light, by rays-in-rays,
Into man's universal reason plays,

4

For wisdom that is vision.—What thou wilt,
    Ask, in the Word-faith, ask and so receive.
Word-faith, the lightning scepter, grasp its hilt,
    Hold up to Christus-Christa : breaths that weave
Through Deity our prayers lead swift reply :
Open the sight to sky transcending sky.

5

Flashes of truth, the lightning of the Word,
    Illuminate the consciousness, then thunders.
Hear the deep, organed bass that, to the third
    From the fourth fullness, leaps while nature sunders.
Thrown for our sight dimensions twain to one ;
Space led through space, God Father in God Son.

6

Touch to the twainness; feel the interplay.
 The greater and the lesser heavens achord.
'Tis thus I fashion this foreshowing lay,
 Lifted through flesh in noon-tide to the Lord.
'Tis so I touch the vibrant judgment bell,
That chimes for paradise, where self makes hell.

PART THIRD

" The sufferings of this present time are not worthy to be
compared with the glory that shall be revealed in us. The
creature was made subject to vanity, not willingly, but by
reason of Him who hath subjected the same in hope; because
the creature itself shall be delivered from the bondage of cor-
ruption into the glorious liberty of the sons of God. Ourselves
also, which have the first fruits of the Spirit, groan within
ourselves, waiting for the adoption, to wit, the redemption of
the body."

ROM. VIII. 18—23.

CONVERSATION IN HEAVEN.

LIV.

1

THE motion of the time is all too fast
    For long persistence.   Life is slow and sweet;
Judgment becomes Repose; its shadows, cast
    To find the ending, rest beneath the feet.
Lives into lives infolding, men are free,
Each in the other's new-born infancy.

2

Feel the repose.   When final chains are broken,
    That held mankind in bondage to the third,
'Twill be as if Deliverance rose, awoken
    To fold the saved in fourthness of the Word.
All who survive, led through the last event,
Unite in free consensus of consent.

3

The end brings quietude, in calm assurance
    That God Twain-One shall nevermore remove.
No more the painful striving for endurance,
    No coiling serpent and no bleeding dove.
Doubt vanishes; indifference is unknown;
Each feels the other's heart his very own.

4

That which men hoped for from the fact of death,
    That which men battled for in anguished strife,
That which men vaguely felt through shadowed faith,
    Is realized in one new fact, New Life.
Men died not, simply it was death that died :
We live, but in the One-Twain glorified.

5

'Tis a new world evolved through consciousness ;
    Not as the old ; the former things are fled.
The vision of the Loving Loveliness,
    Through woman's life in man's, disperses dread
And fear of loss and change and grief and thrall ;
Griefs melt away as music's dying fall.

6

The Loving Loveliness !   Her effluence laves
    The voice, with flowings for the living speech ;
Language, reborn, celestial from the graves,
    Moves by rich, undulating swells that reach
To thrill and penetrate the common ear,
As Christus spake for Lazarus to hear.

LV.

1

The better life in poesy is killed.
    Minstrelsy fails, as prophecy before ;
Yet men, from song's rich treasury, would gild
    Time's wasted forehead with new spangled ore.
Browning and Tennyson ! alas, the blind
Song Samsons to the idol's pillars bind.

2

With storms of melody the walls were shaken ;
  Carlylean thunders melted in the strains ;
Yet in Delilah's chain their lives were taken ;
  The verse was wrought of shadows and remains.
The fictile woman imaged in the third
Held them, dream-spelled, bound from the Bridal Word.

3

Saint John would chant a new apocalypse ;
  Saints Michael and Ithuriel forge new spears ;
Saint Dante draw from Beatrice's lips
  Wine of such melody as charms the spheres ;
Saint Böehme and Saint Swedenborg prolong,
Through lives of rhythmic fire, the Lord's new song ;

4

The music-breathing horses of the sun
  Whirl the song-motion by Apollo's wheels ;
Yea, Lyric Heavens, by all their lives twain-one,
  Tone for new ages, whilst old time repeals.—
Vain, vain ! where Browning, Tennyson but fail,
Barred gates of silence 'gainst the Word prevail.

5

Dear poets, whose melodious hearts were beakers,
  They could not brim though Christa poured the wine :
They dwelt enthralled amid the pleasure seekers ;
  Their tents were pitched where Circe fools her swine :
They kissed Delilah ; felt their locks divide ;
Toiled in smooth ego's fetter-house, and died.

6

Heart, heart, thou shalt not break in the suppression.
   God-life, new life, wake in the breathing numbers.
Think through the fourthness to the song's confession;
   Loose the pent fire, in melody that slumbers.
Christ's lyric lance must penetrate the curled
Self-dragon,—Michael, fighting for the world.

LVI.

1

Through breathful quietude the motion floweth
   That leads the Song Word to its revolution.
'Tis by its minstrelsy the Spirit goeth
   That liberates the heavens for evolution.
Judgment, who bathes in rest for new attire,
Leads the song's action by etheric fire.

2

I sat in Mother Judgment's banquet hall.
   There were twelve Poets at the table round,
And She was manifest to each in all,
   Through their twelve brides, all as Her lilies crowned.
To each through all She passed by swift returns,
Brimming their hearts from Her melodious urns.

3

A roseate splendor canopied the feast;
   Each in the others tasted bosom bread,
And sacred nectars, that for cheer increased,
   Multiplied to them as they quaffed and fed;
But, when the banquet ended, for retire
They led a joy-dance, whilst One played the lyre.

4

He seemed the minstrel of some ancient king.
  Sweet gladness interflowed them, breasting through ;
Twelve stars of radiation glimmering
  Robed them in color as when morn is new ;
So twelve-in-twelve they woke a song of glee
In the dance-music. "this is He, is He !"

5

Thus the Lord Christus manifested there ;
  Yet, manifesting, so diffused His robe
That the twelve poets each took on to wear
  The semblance that was His upon the globe ;
Whilst, from His ancient habitude unvailed,
Christus rose in them and the song prevailed.

6

Thence afterward He oped to them twelve chambers,
  Each in the Lady Christa's holy house :
One body in such apostolic members,
  Twelve, each one-twain, bride with her sacred spouse,
And, while He blest them by the wand and rod,
They folded to sweet rest in One-Twain God.

LVII.

1

"Signs of the Son of Man" appeared in heaven,
  When Swedenborg the seer, by intromission,
Saw the closed scripture of old Israel riven,
  And fourth dimensioned light break through to vision.
Wise, manly, simple, virtuous and sincere,
New spring, through sad old autumn, caught his ear.

2

So, in time's withered foliage round him drifted,
　　He felt to buds that secret blossoms nursed :
Vails after vails that closed the Mother lifted ;
　　Judgment upon his lips the advent versed ;
Apostles on white steeds from heaven outrode
T'ward the far earth ; exultantly they trode.

3

Prophetic, yet for prophecies that arrowed,
　　Not rounded to the compass of the sphere,
He saw that third dimensioned times were narrowed ;
　　The "Heavenly Jerusalem" full near.
Whilst Europe lapped in luxury and decline,
He met the tempest, hastening to the line.

4

The nineteenth century's latter half, he thought,
　　Would feel the Holy City in descent.
So the New Church, all in a mirage caught,
　　Figured before for the divine event.
Through language oft pedantic, hard, full stone,
The Worded lightning by him spake and shone.

5

I saw him in the Mother's blissful palace,
　　Bathed all in merriment, his heart a-flow,
Whilst words escaped his lips in joyful sallies.
　　Four gracious ladies posed as one, to grow
Into a round white girl before his eyes :
Through her the Goddess opened by surprise.

6

She touched him on his full conjugial chin,
   Called him a name of preciousness, and fed
His bosom with delightsome airs, to win
   A wisdom to his brow: 'twas then he said,
"Mother-in-Father, in Thy flesh I feel
The spiritual sense, but by the heel.

7

"It presses on mankind's vulgarity;
   Whilst from the dimples of the rosy skin
A vortice—God in solidarity—
   Whirls down to spiral the vile city's din.—
Now Peter, Peter!"—at the call drew nigh
One crucified of yore head down to die.

8

"Now Peter," thus the wiser babe spake on,
   "Now Peter, tell me if thy bird will crow."
Peter flung forth a bird his brow upon,
   And rippling laughter caught him soon and so;
But the apostle gravely said, "I preach:
Morn's clarion bird is more than any speech.

9

"Could but this fowl perch on men's brows below,
   And flash new morning through their optic sense,
And scatter bridal dews of Lilimo'
   From his brave wings, to cool their fierce offense,
And trumpet where they in denial stand,
They might awake to Judgment in their land."

8

10

The sage stood silent ; swift the vision passed.
    Again the four wise ladies nigh him stood ;
One after one their vails upon him cast,
    Till four-fold splendors robed him,—truth in good.
His flesh absorbed the mantles, and their blaze
Robed him as naked innocence arrays.

11

Being thus clad, he worshiped ; giving thanks
    For the Divine so manifest that day.
A pleasant stream, that wound twixt flowery banks,
    Drew him into the wavelets by a play,
And rising there its naiad met his side,
A maiden of the Truth-well, now his bride.

LVIII.

1

To ask a blessing of the Lord One-Twain,
    The attitude is high straightforwardness.
Say what you think and feel by meanings plain ;
    Then leave it ; never importune or press.
Remember, all good gifts are given for ends
Of human good ; speak as to Faithful Friends.

2

In Shinto worship, knelt before a mirror,
    The Japanese approach by open breast,
Seeking that every stain of fault or error
    May be exposed, revealed and thus confest.
Seek to be mirrored into God, that so
The purities of truth may interflow.

3

'Tis purity of purpose, led to sense
   Through all the avenues of mind and heart,
That holds the vital ethers to condense,
   Force, freedom, courage, fullness to impart,
Till purity is fashioned to a band
Of living steel, a weapon for the hand.

4

Angels are all in childlike innocence.
   Such innocence, to heroism led,
Guides the new man to breathful dominance ;
   Persistence in him, through him, to him wed.
Full prayer's full answer must in this consist,
Wisdom to know, that service may persist.

5

The Word by fourthness through our being plies.
   I saw in Mother's house the " wishing gate."
Four Wishers fashioned there to meet the eyes ;
   The four to show One Lady rose elate ;
Wove wingéd robes without, within ; but soon
Floated beyond, seen as the Judgment Moon.

6

Judgment is God-wish in particulars,
   Orbed to a universal for the globe ;
Hence every wish, in one desire of Hers,
   Is wrought to outline an etheric robe,
Textured so fine that not the tiniest mote
Of the world's ill may through its meshes float.

7

But, through such woven orb, Her wishes flying
    Glide as swift sounds of music's vital scale;
With rise and fall, wish unto wish replying,
    To penetrate the furious passion gale
Of egoistic wishes, base, unkind,
Led from the frenzied, fatuous mankind.

8

In Ego's wish-world aye originate
    The fires that desolate, the blasts that smite
Young eden, that the Word-Truth would create,
    From the small wishes that are God's delight.
The smallest wish is pregnant with its will,
That grows by time to vanish, or fulfill.

9

There was a mirror in that Lady's hand
    Whom I have loved and worshiped from my youth;
So, looking in it, I beheld a band
    Of infants, each an innocence of truth.
She spake, "these are My wishes, hived in thee."—
"Heaven lies about us in our infancy,"

10

Sang Poet Wordsworth.—So, as I remember,
    A wistful child grown to but three years' size,
I woke one dawn-tide in a lone white chamber,
    And sportive fairies danced before mine eyes,
Gold clad, gold winged, form, feature, motion won
From living light-beams, infants of the sun.

11

"Heaven lies about us in our infancy";
   Hence heaven may touch the eyes for impregnation,
And in the mind beget a progeny
   Of wishes, multiply a fairy nation.
Thus Heaven may from the first within us grow;
Its " New Jerusalem " descending so.

LIX.

1

Not half the water, that the miller sees
   Glide in his flume, may serve to turn the wheel.
Not half the interfluent melodies
   The poet feels may in his verse reveal.
Not half the heroes to the wars who go
The triumph hail, nor bind the conquered foe.

2

Results are hidden in the summer's path;
   The ripened seeds for after seasons rise.
Time's glacial ages buried in cold wrath
   Germs to bud forth for future paradise.
Truths may unfold through poets, now and then,
From seed that fell in eden's garden glen.

3

Exalt the Infinite Economy;
   Live in it, serve in it and by it thrive.
Changed heavens and hells to an autonomy
   Inweave; that coming aions may derive,
For ampler systems of the human kind,
Angels made flesh, in heroisms twined.

4

The sparrows fall, yet not one birdling flutters
   To dust beyond the Father-Mother sight.
The Word, made Song, to us the truth re-utters;
   The Infinite Economists delight
In breeding, through all loss, the priceless gain.
No psychic germ of man is born in vain.

5

Excess of waters, from the miller's flume,
   Sweeps on to serve the lilies of the linn.
Excess of music, from the minstrel's loom,
   Weaves living sympathies to fold us in.
Excess of heroes, from one People's throe,
Robes Victory in a crimson after-glow;

6

Rising to meet the sunrise, and to make
   Freedom's new day more glorious. They unprison;—
Souls that are clarions for God's lips awake,—
   In heroisms wake, for triumphs risen.
I saw the Mother as Diana go,
The Virgin Huntress armed with spear and bow.

7

Eve's glowing crescent o'er Her forehead shone;
   The luminous white ether was Her robe.
Emergent, gliding from Her silver throne,
   Arisen heroes wrought the orbing globe,
And, in associated valor dight,
Diffused warm courage for time's lower night.

8

Judgment, as Valor in the innocent,
   'Nears, the world's animosities to stem :
'Tis thus methinks the Heavens are in descent :
   Only they come as Judgment moves in them ;
But She includes them all, cathedral-wise,
In the orb-temple of Her sanctities.

LX.

1

Nature is all a moving allegory ;
   In symbols all the third dimension stands,
Waiting till men shall comprehend her story,
   Finding the Word Truth leaning o'er her bands.
The scripture of the ages forms and plies,
Winged to upbear free manhood for the rise.

2

Yet third dimensioned minds but scan the scripture,
   And third dimensioned lives but scripture feel,
Caught in the shaded allegoric texture.
   Revealment doth not all its Word reveal ;
The affluent mansion, by its lavish store,
Conceals the Master, who is yet the "Door."

3

The Door is everywhere : Word omnipresent
   Invites each passer-by to be a guest ;
Scholar and simplist, pontiff, bard and peasant.
   Scripture is woven for our nightly rest ;
Scripture the basis of our worlded stay ;
The moving firmament that spans our way.

4

Read Swedenborg anew with larger thought;
  For Hebrew scrolls, that met his visioned sense,
Peruse the universe in symbols wrought;
  Find there the immanent Omniscience.
Man's form, the microcosm, holds inscaled
The Flying Form of God, yet unrevealed.

5

The Jewish lattice opened to the star.
  For lattice claim the firmament; look through
Time's universe to Christ in avatar;
  From thirdness into fourthness thus pursue;
Find God, thy Morn, through oriented eyes.
Thou art a scripture, man, the Word supplies,

6

Through each fine organ of thy four-fold frame,
  Fire-substance of free being; taste and see:
Find God, the Vital Fire that feeds thy flame.
  Thou art ingermed, involved in Deity.
For re-creation of thy form of shells,
O'ercome the hostile ego that repels.

7

God the Imaginer imagined earth:
  The universe grew from imagination.
In past, in present and in everforth,
  Word, the Revealer, fills the revelation;
Yet vails therein, free creatures to invite,
And form them to God's likeness of delight.

8

God the Imaginer imagined thee ;
  Else thou an imaged likeness hadst not been.
God is the Secret of the mystery,
  That vails thy human consciousness within.
That mystery, closed in earthly common place,
Seeks to transform thee to its form of grace ;

9

To wing thee for angelical advances ;
  To voice thee in the paradisal choirs,
And lead thee through the hymeneal dances ;
  Enrobing thee in the etheric fires.
A wingéd germ, seed of the Word, art thou ?
That Word is thine ; the breath-wind woos thee now.

10

I pause,—a man in all who suffer smitten ;
  A voice, through buffetings that breasts the gale ;
A flying flame, yet by the Word-fire litten ;
  Voice, flame and presence fugitive and frail.—
The vision overcomes me ; songs that burn
Find silence in my bosom by return.

11

A mortal may o'ercome mortality ;
  Scriptures rise glorified, orbed in their Word ;
Freedom put on divine fatality ;
  Fulfilment battle on, through hopes deferred,
To rest where bridal vails from heaven are spun.
Lord Christus guides the horses of the sun.

LXI.

1

Each house I dwell in proves a prison house,
   Peopled with pains and compassed by the grave.
Ego's worst dominance at last avows ;
   Truth's firmest freeman now is lowliest slave.
1 search the planet for a spot of rest ;—
Not one, each holds a dagger to the breast.

2

The truth of love, of reason and of act,
   The New Life's martyr anguish, and its risen
Persistence, all of potencies compact,
   Serve but to make the groaning earth their prison.
I stand as one upon a lifting reef,
Whelmed by the universal unbelief :

3

For ego now is growing pestilential :
   Its pestilence the cultured mind invades.
Illusions overcome the evidential,
   For God has set ; night moves in falling shades.
The gate is barred ; Christus, who is our door,
Is closed upon ; the opening shows no more.

4

Ego, the planet's ghastly poisoner,
   Sets loose all airs of mortal ills that are,
To crush the senses that for God-life stir ;
   To whirl our wasting bodies o'er the bar
Of dissolution to the hungry waves.
Judgment but enters to emerge through graves.

5

Pains through the winds are woven ; pains uplift
　Where'er the feet on sacred errands go.
The human waters hold the icy drift ;
　Each sentient structure chills to meet the flow :
Sense-thought in godness feels its nerves uncoil ;
Feels dissolution of its powers make spoil.

6

Yet ego's mind enjoys inanity.
　There was a " wise one " talked last eve with me ;
His thoughts were shells, their instinct vanity,
　Yet as a self-created god spake he ;
" Christus an earlier comrade at the most :
Himself god, father, son and holy ghost."

7

" Yea, ye shall be as gods "; such gods are they
　As specters are, that through death's dream-doors flutter;
Glow-worms that simulate the starred array ;
　Bats who shrill cries from fetid caverns utter.
Creeds, cultures, sciences and arts enlarge,
Shaping fool ego to such last discharge.

8

Such theosophical illusions lent
　A specious color to old Egypt, when
The faith of Osiris and Isis went
　Down to its hades, lost, forgotten then.
Such passed for ruin o'er the Roman world,
Ere the barbarian hydra crushed and curled.

9

To flaunt the utter godlessness of God ;
    To shape the final manlessness of men ;
To couch the occult in a devious fraud ;
    Rewrite the Past with Fiction for a pen,
And swing the torch that lures to ruin's shore,
Ego, grown theosophic, bars the "Door."

10

Rome whirled in conflagration ; Nero fiddled.
    This theosophic ego views the fire
That whelms Society, begrimed, bedeviled,
    And plays its pipe for idiots to admire ;
Then whispers, where the topmost blaze has clomb,
"It is the Christians who set fire to Rome."

11

Yet they who hold the fourthness dare the grip
    Of the envenomed octopus ; nor bide
In himalay, to bid the war dogs slip
    Who bay at Christus, bleeding, crucified.
Subtlest of foes are they who last we meet,
Aroused where Truth leads to the judgment seat.

LXII.

1

Souls in the ego swallowed up, and given
    To the full egoistic, mind and will,
Efface the form and portraiture of heaven,
    And, for the Living Word, with semblance fill :
As intellectual phantoms they dispread ;
Void images of manhood that is fled.

2

" What shall it profit to a man if he
   Gain the whole world and lose his soul thereby" ?
The seeming man, a vain self-deity,
   Subsists in pretence, an organic lie.
Ego, the occupant, his content flows ;
Gilding the surface, shaping to its close.

3

As a "mahatma" he may posture so ;
   Subversive evolution for his art :
He may project a doubled selfness ; go,
   By "astral forms," in nature's occult part ;
Build magic to a fortress and a shrine,
And subject mortals to his purpose twine.

4

In self-idolatry grown absolute,
   He may assume the philanthropic dress ;
Priest, ruler, scholar ; pluck the planet's fruit,
   Aloof in a secretive lordliness ;
Weave nature through his glamour for a spell ;
Move panoplied in seeming miracle.

5

Obliterating sex-life from the soul,
   He may emerge as the supreme magician ;
His lore by secret artifice outroll,
   For a religion that is irreligion ;
Dead to all sympathy, in time remain,
Implied in mortal cold and free from pain.

6

In occult third dimension, past the bounds
   Of seen mortality, he may have built
His deadly pleasure house, where nature's wounds
   Are open, and the planet's life is spilt
To streams of wasted vigors, that inflow
The downward growth, a fictioning to show,

7

As mimic eden, tempe, sybaris :
   The oozing breasts of nature heave therein,
Reviving pleasures to a spectral bliss,
   Glancing by wasting fires to light her "Zin,"
Her den of many caverns, where she wiles,
To fold the souls of guile into her guiles.

8

Such their "devachan" by its real fact,
   Where egos rest, and taste by emanation
Pleasures that from past earthliness re-act ;
   Dream on to think the close re-incarnation.
This is the hidden source, whose flowings pour
To earth for ego-theosophic lore.

LXIII.

1

There is a Borderland, not Heaven nor Hell,
   Where souls, all spell-bound by the earth's attraction,
As shells or phantoms find their greater shell
   In failure, fraud, fatuity and faction.
'Tis mirage, image ; changeful gleams refract
From Time's huge comedy and tragic act.

2

" Mediums" are peep-holes in the shadowed curtain,
   And "sensitives" are fingers for the feel.
Uncertainties thus imitate the certain ;
   Ghost-babble takes on knowings to reveal.
'Tis parasitical : the psychic flies
Buzz to mankind ; 'tis here their feeding lies.

3

" Seek ye the Lord while yet He may be found,"
   And ego be coerced to disappear.
Be not beguiled through fact in falsehood bound ;
   The crystal pendant in the specter's ear.
When Hades earthward lifts to cast her dead,
Judgment has troubled her, the darts are sped.

4

Nirvana's path is through the city streets,
   Where'er the men of rescue hold their might ;
Where'er God's heart through heaven-born pity beats ;
   Where'er the holy dove is found in flight ;
Where'er the heart's new touch to God begins
By love that leads forgiveness of the sins.

5

Ego-theosophist, lo ! he denies
   Christ the Forgiver ;—be it so to him.
Nature needs no forgiveness, but she dies,
   Lost as the wine drop from the beaker's brim.
Who hath not sinned, betrayed by ego's lust ?
In the Forgiver of the sins we trust.

6

"Grace did the more abound where sin abounded":
   'Tis grace that wings the Incarnation on.
Men by sin's consequents are hurt and hounded:
   Christ the Defender bids the fault "begone";
Imputes His righteousness, instilled to grow
And fill the life, assimilated so.

7

Savior, in Thee we trust! 'tis Saviorism
   First, last and always, that our faith invites.
The race is mazed in ego's fateful schism;
   Ours be the "path," in Him who re-unites.
"Survival of the fit"?—the fit are they,
Repentant, who believe and who obey.

LXIV.

1

"Strike while the iron is hot"; the hammer ply;
   'Tis thus dull ore transforms to piercing dart.
Pause not for flaming sparks that near thee fly;
   Christus the Workman nerves thee for thy part.
I saw in Judgment's labor hall again
Christus, the Workfellow of workingmen.

2

Gold mist His mighty forehead overhung;
   Gold sweat in globules shone upon His breast;
His nerved right arm a massive hammer swung.
   A melody in harmony, a rest
In labor, so His utterance became;
A sweetness led to flow in fiery flame.

3

"Take thou no thought, but in the Word abide,
  For so shapes throughness in thee to a gift.
Lift thou the ponderous truth, to life applied,
  In thy small way, as I this hammer lift:
It falls to break the iron-hearted shell
Of ego, in whose mass the Word-seed dwell."

4

The verse rose heaving in me, as full rain
  Of fire when thunderbolts to flame are beaten.—
The vision changed; I saw the One-in-Twain,
  When precious wine was poured and viands eaten.
Twelve men of labor, crowned with garlands gay,
'Feasted one-twain as wedded lovers may.

5

Seen as the Publican, the Lord sat there,
  Beaming, on hospitable cares intent;
With Mother Christa in a twain-one chair
  Of wicker work, in knots and garlands bent;
But, like a table waitress fair to view,
A daughter served, known here as "Lady Sue."

6

Out from a single bowl rolled cups and dishes;
  Forth from one glass the crystal goblets wrought.
One fish grew on the board to twelve twain fishes;
  One loaf to twelve came forth as thoughts from thought.
Then the Lord smiled, while tenderly he spake,
"Ye labor, and I labor for your sake.

9

7

"Wherever twelve as ye shall sit at table
  In the new time, I will purvey the feast.
They who subserve shall be for godness able
  To lead new vigors to the lowest least;
And I will make my presence in the wolds
Of earth for pleasances and for strong-holds.

8

"So We shall keep the labor feast in sightness
  Of such as ye; for joyance meeting them,
To lead the dance by feet of flying lightness.
  I am the Root of Labor, and the stem
Shall from me rise and branch, and bear increase
Of infants, orbed in righteousness and peace."

LXV.

1

Lord Christus claims the right to "live the Life"
  On earth; the right denied to Him of yore,
Peace and good will to all, no chain or strife.
  He claims the freedom of the planet's floor,
To live the life, to breathe unfettered breath
As Man in man: such is the word He saith.

2

Of old his posture was below mankind.
  Now on the level of the race He stands;
In the equalities would be enshrined;
  In the fraternities would fashion hands.
In liberty, for liberties, His will
Is postured; He would work no creature ill.

3

Let whoso live who holds the right to live;
  Let whoso die who holds the cause to die.
No act of His shall any man deprive
  Of aught that is an human equity.
Let all who choose of independence boast;
He seeks no rule or presence in their host.

4

Let all who will compete; He will not strive
  To check the freedom of their competition;
Nor touch the reins their purposes to drive;
  Nor force their thought; but hold His free position
In simple Manliness; a Citizen
Of the republic, seen or viewless then.

5

The right to free expression, act and motion
  He comes to claim; nor will assert for more.
He sought mankind by purposeful devotion;
  Now men must seek Him, being still the Door.
To live the life, to show it by its worth,
For this He immanates to human earth.

6

Men need not fear for an authority;
  Nor shall authority His freedom bind.
Accepting here the fact, democracy,
  His entrance stirs no ripple on the wind
Of their free motion; He but aids events
That fashion in the movement of consents.

7

He will not press a good however good;
    Nor jar upon an ill however ill.
Let this for first time now be understood,
    He comes His Social Manhood to fulfill:
He does not move in cataclysmal storm,
But as the sunbeam ;—let who will be warm.

8

He claims the right to form association,
    As He with those who draw to Him shall woo;
To hold estate, to serve the occupation,
    Doing to all as all to Him should do;
Seeking thereby to cause no just offense
To tribe or nation, spirit, mind or sense.

9

He claims the right that Keely has besought,
    To wake etheric force by timed vibration;
The right that Edison has almost caught,
    To lead swift ethers to illumination;
The right that held Columbus to pursue
And on the old world's confines twine the new.

10

He has no dogma to defend or proffer:
    Truth must from life to evolution flow.
He will not lavish from a private coffer
    Favors, to buy as those who bribes bestow.
The third dimension opens for His play;
He enters it to walk His four-fold way.

11

So all who will to tread the path with Him
  May move, as best befits, to His right hand.—
Turn to the Right!—earth-time is growing dim;
  The light to come in Him will o'er them stand.
Away the foolish babble, paltry strife;
Christ comes to live in those who live the life.

LXVI.

1

September's balmy lips again are breathing,
  To woo the sense, from odorous retreats.
Mild, pensive autumn glides, before her wreathing
  Cool, dewy vapors, lost in lingering heats.
Entrancing glances, kisses of farewells,
Touch to the heart.   Departure with us dwells.

2

Now hastes the close of Heaven's industrial year,
  That with the rainy equinox began.
In fourth dimensioned ripeness re-appear
  To worded sight the groves of Lilistan.
In a grand pleasure park, upon its mall,
I met a man, last of the twelve, Saint Paul.

3

"Taste of my fruit" he spake, "last of the season;
  Upon a bough of Christ's first tree it hung."
Sharp acid was its taste, a fruit of reason
  In eloquence, upon the lip it clung.
I answered, joining with him in the cheer,
'Taste of my fruit, the first of Christ's new year.'

4

"This is a fruit of wisdom in conviction,"
    Quoth he replying, "ah! it holds God's wine,
The Bridegroom's breath, a nuptial benediction:
    I share it joyful with this spouse of mine."
A tall bright lady youthful as nineteen,
His spouse was visioned, stately, grecian seen.

5

He wound an arm around her lissome waist,
    With " Phœbe sweetest, one-in-twain we are.
Young gospel, love is exquisite in taste;
    Scriptured are you in Christa's avatar."
Her wifely thought into his own she crost,
Then Paul exclaimed "Time passes, time is lost.

6

"The power, the glory and the majesty
    Of Christ Twain-One, all thought of time excelling,
Transposes time; so time is winged to fly
    Into God's bosom. Ends the vague foretelling:
Now shall the autumn of the age exhaust
In Spring's new rain, first imaged as white frost."

7

My palm he touched with apostolic fervor;
    Trembled as virgins on the delphic seat;
Spake, "did I well, in Christ our God, to serve Her
    The Goddess; worshiping the Paraclete?"
One mirrored named as "Chloe," a white flame
Of wifely womanhood, a pure unshame.

8

She breathed upon his lips to leave an answer.
   Then shone his eyes, twin stars from truth's deep well,
"Did I conceive of Her as no romancer?
Wrought She into my thought a sacred spell?
Unto my simple mind did She incline,
She who is Grace and Graciousness Divine?"

9

Chloe began, "Paul-Paula, brother-sister,"
   But Phœbe spake, "the Comfortress impoured
Through Chloe's faithfulness; our Paulus kissed Her,
   The Mother, sprinkled from the Bridal Word.
In the epistle to the Romans then
He wrought Her scripture, though with failing pen.

10

"Grace, grace his theme, led from our Gracious Lady;
   His was the grecian in the jewish car."—
The three upon my sight grew dim and shady;
   More hence was said that is untimely here.
Smile, kind September: where thy footsteps fall
Angels glide in thee, Paula and her Paul.

LXVII.

1

I met a shaker priestess, Anna Girling,
   Met in a shadowed glen below our mall;
She was indulging in a pious whirling,
   Watched prudently by Paula one with Paul.
She gave a recognizing glance, with "you
Say that the angels all are one in two.

2

"Nay, nay, Christ is our bridegroom, sole and purely;
  He is contained within my holy roll;
In it I feel his presence near and hourly,
  The sacred spouse, the lover of my soul.
So all the sister spirits with me tell,
That he their precious bridegroom is as well."

3

Oddly, there stepped anigh a shaker Elder,
  Drew a long sigh: she called him by a name,
And, when into his glance he drew and held her,
  A smoldering fire within them broke to flame.
Again the whirl, but now with hands that crost
And feet that flew, till from them shone white frost.

4

The cold of celibacy, in them nursed
  By chill religion whilst their time held years,
Lay as dull snow upon their flesh; dispersed
  To icy vapor, flowed to faints and fears;
But each, the other holding so to cling,
From Paula-Paul drew kindly comforting.

5

They touched each other's fingers as to feel,
  But timidly with ague pains forlore;
Till the good shaker turned upon his heel,
  Turned full from Anna and his garment tore,
Crying, "I testify; the feel I had
Affirms within me; woman, you are bad."

6

She rose indignant, with the tart reply,
  "Nay, nay! 'tis Christ within me doth affirm
That thou art given to believe a lie,
  And verily a servant of the worm.
Did I know somewhat of a man or two?
Begone, I testify, I spit on you."

7

So after "testifying" both sat down,
  Panting, exhausted by such verbal pass.
The elder, looking with a piteous frown,
  Austerely droned, "yea, yea, I loved a lass.
Somewhat in you recalled the thought of her,
And then old Adam in me 'gan to stir."

8

Paul queried of him, "was it not New Adam?
  Did you not feel to her as pure young Eve?"
Both rose, addressed first time as "Sir" and "Madam,"
  As gentleman and lady who receive,
Till Anna, like a conscious maid from school,
Colored and sighed, then spake, "I am a fool.

9

"I knew you, from the first, for just the picture
  Of my dear bridegroom in the holy roll,
And loved and dreaded, with a joyous mixture
  Of feelings almost past my heart's control."—
"Love one another," doves awoke to coo
From Paula's bosom, "sweetest, I love you."

LXVIII.

1

Eternities in times unite for us,
  To lead the spectacle that rounds the play.
I saw the star of stars that fights for us,
  Orb Jupiter, as eyes inworded may.
One of that planet's heaven drew kindly near,
By respiration led to brain from ear.

2

Hero and poet, priest and archimage,
  Four-fold his aspect, man of many feels.
Through the prone shadows of earth's mortal age,
  A splendor motioned from him, wheels in wheels
Of wingéd thoughts; the thoughts to me became
As flying cherubs, orbed in solar flame.

3

Four men stood with me by an interbreath,
  Paul, Peter, James and John: formed to unite,
We met the vision, not as from beneath,
  But on the level of transposive sight.
Thus holding eye to eye, at one with them,
John spake, "this place is New Jerusalem.

4

"To priesthood, kingship, scienthood and song
  The inspirations of the Life converge."
Paul spake, "to four-fold ladyhoods belong
  The leading powers that for the gifts emerge.
The Gracious Lady holds, the bands between;
Through Her the star that heralds day is seen."

5

Spake Peter, "lo! She is the Shepherdess,
   And all the stars of heaven are in Her flock.
I touch the key-note of Her holiness;
   Then doors of New Jerusalem unlock
To sacred entrances, divine arcades:
Her palace there is in Her white robed maids."

6

Spake James, "and priests with jewelled garments clothen."
   "And poets chanting blithely," spake Saint John;
"Their vestures all in melody are woven:
   As to their brows, the white dove plumes thereon,
And lips are sweet, impassioned to bestow
Songs in the Mother's praise from Lilimo'."

7

"Imputed to them all such righteousness,"
   Spake Paul; "it is the Lord's, thus made their own.
To Her in Him assimilate, they press
   The lips of holiness for blessings known.
'Tis wrought to form and fill and flow and fall;
The Bridegroom's marriage robe enfolding all."

8

"Blessed are they," spake four in one together,
   "Who to the marriage feast of Christ are led."—
Through the dim haze of time, its closing weather,
   The palpitating airs of heaven are fed;
Breathing to hearts that for Him yearn the most
Far whisperings of the apostolic host.

LXIX.

1

The planet mellows like a fallen fruit;
  Nature's last ripeness presses on mankind;
The year holds many years in swift pursuit,
  All urging on the final goal to find.
All human lives, around the orb that spin,
Weave narrowing circles: time is folding in.

2

Note the massed fishes crowded in a seine;
  Nearing the beach they rush to 'scape the net.
Minds whom the thirdnesses of space restrain
  Make frantic toil to burst the billowing fret.
Men as the captive fish are caught in fear,
Or insects when hoar frost invades the year.

3

'Tis not the shapen thought, 'tis thought unshapen
  That holds the mortal situation now.
That which men vaguely feel is Visitation;
  A moving Future, vailed from feet to brow,
Whose bosom palpitates to thrill the air
Of the world's thought, urging by tremors there.

4

Faiths, finances and morals are afloat:
  Legends, laws, ligatures are failed or failing;
Fierce war-hawks whirling o'er the mortal cote,
  And hungry sharks anear the swimmer sailing.
Butchers are rulers o'er the wattled folds,
And anarchy a-foot in the strong-holds.

5

Time's Giant feels to shake his prison doors,—
   The fierce flame-giant of Democracy.
'Tis not the human voice, a tempest roars.
   Peoples that are not peoples, but a sea
Of hungers, furies, whetted fangs in fears,
Would riot in a ruin that anears.

6

Ah me! what shouts of maddened indignation
   Ascend for antichrist's millennial reign;
Sin's ignomy; the impious desecration
   Of Freedom, trampling order in disdain;
The carnival of ego, free to swing,
With Lust for queen and Violence for king.

7

'Tis this or that; the mortal ego lifted,
   All good to smite, all evil to uprear;
Or else the Holy City, deathless, gifted
   Four-fold in grace of godness to appear.
Man cannot cleave the mesh with gordian knife;
All waits upon the coming of the Life.

LXX.

1

The mystery of Woman's life is deep.
   A flowing ocean, azure, crystalline,
She holds the sanctity of Christ to keep,
   Since in her heart of hearts is Christa's shrine.
The rose of her pure holiness adorns
His bosom who for her was crowned with thorns.

2

I touched a lady's finger, that she gave,
   In a small nook of Lady Yessa's bowers.
Her presence rose upon me as a wave
   From the inflowing sea; her breasts were towers.
Espoused to Christ? I knew it by the ring
She held to meet my sight, thus witnessing.

3

A wingéd whiteness, snowy swan of swans,
   She billowed on the air-way for the sight.
'Twas thus I met the Maid of Orleans ;
   She who won France to freedom, by the might
Of God-force, when the land was torn apart,
And Britain ruled from battle-field to mart.

4

But thereupon twelve mighty men of valor
   Encompassed her : here is a truth for us ;
Whereas she moved enshrined in sacred pallor,
   They, for the grace that flowed, shone glorious.
Such maid of Christ infuses through the host,
By fiery baptism of the Holy Ghost.

5

Yet for such worth she drank the bitter draught.
   The price she paid was martyrdom, the stake,
The curling flame : noting my thought she laughed
   Shook, as from bosomed swan, a floating flake,
That held her answer drifting to mine eyes;
"Warm hearted woman triumphs when she dies."

6

Strange if an inspiration should defeat
   Its final purposes, when led a-field
By heroism in the bravest sweet.
   Strange that the victress should as victim yield
Her sacred flesh, to feed the fiery thirst
Of enmities, that wrought their last and worst;

7

But stranger that a simple peasant maid
   Should lift a nation from its ruining.
'Twas Grace, in lowly womanhood arrayed;
   'Twas Liberty, in her upon the wing;
The Goddess of the people kindling so,
Through midnight, for the future's coming glow.

8

For Judgment on a land's despoilers then,
   Whilst Christendom lay in its deepest dark,
The Mother led, four-folding into men:
   This is the mystery of Jeanne d'Arc;
Whereby She wrought in battles, for the way
Of the deliverance, ere yet was day.

9

Judgment looks far before; from such despoilers
   Old Europe's woman land rose liberate,
That fires might breed, to leap through smitten toilers,
   To Revolution for their opening gate.
The Maid of Orleans 'twas who touched the key,
That led the People's rise in "ninety three."

LXXI.

1

Think four-fold to the east, west, north and south;
  Wisdom is in us now for sight grown free.
The bosom of the race is parched with drouth;
  Man shapes a desert where he held a sea.
His poor remains of life are whirled in storms,
Through broken structures, desiccated forms.

2

The flowing Truth his breast would not retain;
  His natural sense the breathing Word repels;
The vital current shows but through a stain,
  Hues, colors vaguely on his vacuous shells.
Truth, for the ages flowing to mankind,
Ceases: it leaves the arid self behind.

3

Now, pressing on where flying Truth has fled,
  Leave the dry wilderness; pursue the flight,
Rise to clear consciousness by Wisdom led;
  Find the new stand-place formed in upper light.
Look four-fold east, west, north and southward; here
In Heaven's full bosom, lo! what floods appear.

4

The desiccated earth-air led dejection;
  Fear, apathy and languor wove and spun,
Till God-thought failed into a recollection,
  And morn seemed but dead morn and dying sun.
The desert heat grew on us, till it lay,
A death-mask, on the face of living day.

5

I met a Sentinel, upon the brink
  Of the etheric heaven's o'erfolding sphere.
He greeted with an hearty "have to drink";
  Touched for a water-flow led through the ear.
The feel of bubbling waters in the brain
Revived me, Worded thought was free again.

6

"In what malarious element ye wade,
  Ye who bear witness in a time forlorn":
Spake the wise Warder, smiting to a shade ;
  Smiting by sound as from a battle horn.
A grim, gaunt, grisly image for His blows
Broke, crumbled ; through its dust a wraith arose,

7

Who, clinging to my outer vail, had risen
  To form upon me and to fetter down,
That so my life might to his greeds be given.
  His visage faced me with a fearful frown.
I made to stoop and lift him, by a thrill
Of force in kindness, but I met a chill,

8

Cold, cold in venom : stumbling to the feet
  He gasped affrighted ; drew his brow to mine ;
Sought by paralysis my touch to meet ;
  Sought by entanglements its force to twine ;
Failed, flung his form below the "astral plane";
To his own kind whirled in an hurricane.
  10

9

"Yea, suffer it to be so now," One spake.
    "I as the Sentinel this gateway keep.
Ye sought to help that man for my dear sake;
    Thinking, so doing, 'twas to feed my sheep.
So he had fastened on your skirts, to fill
His wasting essence from your kind good will."

10

Afterward, through such "Door," I found a space,
    With twelve who guard the access from the deep.
Paul, Peter, James and John again made place,
    In a strong fortress named as "Never sleep":
Thence One through them, with ever thoughtful eyes
O'erwatches where the danger-path implies.

11

'Tis hard, 'tis desperate hard to hold the foot,
    Encountering men of craft and avarice,
Who seek the confidence intent on "loot,"
    As Christ show fashion but as Judas kiss.
'Tis hard to part the last loaf on the board,
Lost from Christ's poor to swell the traitor's hoard.

12

"Yea, suffer it to be so now": such gifts
    Hold Judgment in them, sure to overthrow.
The bread is cast abroad upon the drifts,
    To rise for harvest through dissolving snow.—
I heard a Voice, a twelve-one carol heard;
Song thrilled my bosom from the Bridal Word.

13

Twelve ladies, brides of the apostles they,
    Rocked in a pleasure barge upon a stream,
Or sported where white water lilies lay,
    And wingéd water-babes rose in the gleam
Of God-light from the east, and showered them.
John spake, "such too is New Jerusalem."

14

"Pray to the Lord, but keep the powder dry";
    Ever the shrewd Cromwellian charge we hold.
The inner eye relieves the outer eye,
    For watchfulness when wearied sense must fold.
Slept the tired watchers in that night of doom,
When Christ, our Sunrise, shadowed for the tomb?

15

Now they keep watch, whilst He, within them, guards
    By Truth that never falters, never sleeps;
Till Guile's defenses fall as broken shards,
    And its proud cities lie in pathless heaps.
O'er time's gethsemane the shades descend;
Here is our watch, till God-rise leads the end.

LXXII.

1

Where we advance to thread the obscuration,
    All the wild glamour of the past makes head;
Shaping the complex of civilization;
    Involving life in cerements of the dead.
Truth shows as falseness, falsehood plumes as true;
Impetuous ego storms and ravins through.

2

Did we dare sleep, the hours by death were numbered;
    Did we dare pause, the desert o'er us drive.
Did we dare house, by mortal ties encumbered,
    To hornet's nest would change the ravished hive.
We can but watch; holding in storm by calm,
A brooding kindliness, a breathing balm.

3

I met the Prophet of the " Lamentations,"
    He who saw Israel chained by Babylon.
Clad in a Word-robe of illuminations,
    He broke a roll with me and fed thereon;
Then gave me of it and it tasted well;
I fed on bread of God for Israel.

4

Yet, for the bread, the belly flowed with water,
    And this again was nectar in the veins;
But Jeremiah stood in vails of slaughter,
    Stood prophesying, and he told of rains.
Full Truth by flood was on him, and his theme
Surged on as one who battles with the stream.

5

But after this a mild, sweet genius came,
    All as a zephyr of translucent air,
And touched him to the navel; then the name
    Of Helios-Christus spake as from him there;
Till upwardly his breasts grew summer red,
To tropic heats by respirations wed.

6

And he was borne in breathings upwardly,
  To pass through Yessa's gardens to a glade,
Where the LORD GOD stood in the galaxy,
  And voiceful constellations to Him made
A song of evolution, and a whirl
That winged young paradises to unfurl.

7

And he was caught into the song, and dipped
  His vails of slaughter in a milky flow,
And his breast opened ; but a Lady slipped,
  To fold Him in Her whiteness, and to glow
Upon him in a radiance of full bloom :
She cleft, She whirled him in a pleasure stroom.

8

"She is the Sephira," spake he enafter,
  "She who is hidden in the name of Yod.
She is the Song of Wisdom and the Laughter,
  The Gladness of the gladnesses of God."
Hearing his voice, twelve prophets, born again
To Israel, bowed their heads and breathed "amen!"

9

The prophesyings of the prophets end ;
  The seeings of the seers are interwoven
Through the transcendent ages that foretend ;
  So are their eyes for new-timed God-light cloven.
The vails of the shekinah burn ; they part ;
Show God One-Twain, Man-Woman, heart in heart.

LXXIII.

1

Down looking from the nigh Etheric Heaven,
  To Earth that in dense proprium-vapor swims,
A Worded sight is for perception given ;
  One views the masses but as manikins ;
Whilst here and there a suffering human face
Glows through the death-mist, lit by heavenly grace.

2

The power of hold is that which characters
  These few amid the many ; 'tis the grip
On the divineness ; 'tis the soul that stirs
  Through the formed frame for godly fellowship,
Doing its utmost best to force a way
For human uprightness by night and day.

3

I saw an Ancient of time's golden age,
  Translated there ; holding the planet's youth
In good remembrance ; he its mortal page
  Searching to find the holding-ground of Truth,
The base in organism, that retains
The grace of God in structures of remains.

4

He drew my searching mind with his to fuse ;
  Then I saw many holding to a law
Of honor in their hearts, a law of use,
  That in them breeds a searchfulness, to draw
The mind into a secret watch and ward,
That thought and action may with right accord.

5

Over all such a light was visible;
  But a magnetic darkness o'er the rest,
That flowed the mortal mind and sense to fill,
  And generate within the breeding breast
Swarms of imperious purposes, designs,
Drawn into wingéd reptiles by their lines.

6

The world that is, the world that vails in schism,
  Sundered in motion from the heavenly host,
Must perish when the foul, black magnetism
  Flushes its continent and floods its coast.
"The wage of sin is death," and death in-urns
Wherr the magnetic flow to ashes burns.

7

Hence comes the instantaneous conflagration.
  The opportune that hastes on Judgment waits:
By the attraction of association,
  Heaven-life in mind-stuff so She re-instates.
The magnetism bred by mortal ills
Wastes, leaving vacuum; this with life She fills.

8

Beamed the gold Ancient, drew a touch to mine,—
  Touch to my heart, that answered by a pang.
A thought found utterance, a thought divine,
  Led through the ear as if a clarion rang;
Then through his form a milk-white vapor rolled
That colored on him as enrobing gold.

9

The vapor that shall clothe the air, and span
   The planet, when its magnetisms meet
The Worded fire, and that which seems as man
   But is not, is dissolved in fervent heat,
Is folded in such man as met mine eyes;
The Golden Folk of Time's lost paradise.

LXXIV.

1

Men will survive by openings in the ear,
   The brain held in etheric emanation;
Old thoughts of thirdness, thoughts of chill and fear,
   Led by a vaporous wave to dissipation;   .
Then, through the auditory nerves a-glow,
Songs without words, life songs of Lilimo'.

2

"Touch to my instep;" spake the round white girl,
   Known four-fold, "Daughter, Issa, Lily, Sue."
I touched with reverence, felt white vapors curl.
   She stood four-fold from coronet to shoe,
Robed as the stately woman of the sea,
Air, vapor, flame in flowing melody.

3

"Men shall survive by chastities divine,"
   Spake she, "the consummation of the third.—
Nay, hold in nuptial troth thy heart to mine,
   For thou must in our union find the Word.
Men shall survive who feel, as thou dost feel,
The Goddess by the woman's touch reveal;

4

"Men who revere the sacred virginal;
  Men who abhor the sexual profanation;
Men who think godness to the terminal;
  Who elevate the host in consummation;
Men who adore the Goddess, though afar,
And thrill through all sensation to Her star.

5

"To such, to such, the Bridal Word is given,
  Rock, temple, column, altar and defense.
In the great hour their bodies will inheaven;
  Their silent thought be worlded eloquence.
Dawn shall be on their foreheads, for the light
Of the new time; their lives into it plight.

6

" Stay :—as our Mother rounds the work complete,
  She will destroy unchastity forever.
She will efface the worthless and effete;
  No breast survive but as 'tis made Her mirror.
So they who look from breast to breast behold
Her Worded futures, twain-in-one, unfold."

LXXV.

1

Fox rediscovered Christianity;
  Its force within him broke false ego's might;
So through sectarian profanity
  Shone the twain truths, Christ and the inner light.
Awe-stricken, plain, sweet, simple, godly man,
Etheric rhythms through his being ran.

2

He was a Voice in time's dim wilderness;
  John Baptist, not of water but of fire.
The Living Christ in him he dared confess,
  Clad in such leathern garment for attire.
Kingly in priestliness, nor house nor lands
Were his.—A kingdom fashioned to his hands.

3

Through him the Worded fourth dimension pointed
  A shaft of regal fire, to penetrate
Where Britain's ancient rule, disrupt, disjointed,
  Gave opening for the mightier births of fate.
The concept of Christ's kingdom in his brain
Wrestled for birth, but here in mortal pain.

4

He sought to organize a People here;
  A royal people, priestly in the Lord.—
View to the upward : see that kingdom near,
  A realm where twain-one unities achord.
A little one of Peoples, grown full strong,
It multiplies three centuries along.

5

There gathered England's brightest, bravest, best,
  Baptized into the concept of the Friend.
George Fox, the pivot chief, by worded hest,
  Led forth Christ's bridal order to its end.
On earth the germ rose from the Lord its root:
Now 'tis a tree of heaven in ripened fruit.

6

Enter that kingdom, by the mind's transfusion ;
  Breathe, by love's faith, its mild and friendly airs ;
Withdraw into the silent, sweet seclusion ;
  See to what futures grew the toils and cares.
The " Inner Light," lo! it endiadems
Over a nobler London of the Thames.

LXXVI.

1

George Fox the quaker, now Fidelius Rex,
  In the illuminated brethren thrones,
Holding for gifts of state : see who bedecks
  Such royalty with beauty; who intones
His life in woman-song; so glimpse, between
The curtained lines, Fidelia the queen.

2

House of the thousand windows fronteth east,
  West, north and south, with precious stones inlaid.
Music of sacred lady bands, released
  In billowy flights of doves, such voicings made
As those who heard, enraptured by the hymn,
Might call " the song of choiring cherubim."

3

Here I met Shakspeare, and another one,
  A joyful guest from mortal thrall set free.
'Twas good to greet dear poet Tennyson
  In such blithe realm, in such brave company.
Each wore such favors, wreaths of the white rose,
As royalty unto its guest bestows.

4

And Tennyson smiled cognizant of me,
    For I had stood beside his passing bed ;
With him upon the bar and out at sea ;
    With him thereafter, when the lights were led
Into his vision, and the Lord Twain-One
Dawned on him in a music of the sun.

5

A wingéd one, a radiant Ariel
    With message from more kingly Prospero,
Hovered in air, and, from a dew-lipped shell,
    Poured language that was melody in flow :
It broke as if from diamonded rains
Fell flowers, dissolved to odors in the veins.

6

So through the guest house we were led, to enter
    A lyric hall therein, built temple-wise,
Wherein the four-fold ways to one concenter ;
    The path of Wisdom in her poesies ;
But in it, for its glory, shone a Grace
In Holiness, the Lady of the place.

7

Four-fold her presence ; four-fold choirs, bride-maiden,
    Forth from Her bosom led by four-fold ways,
And cherub boys and girls with garlands laden
    Wreathed us divinely.　To the Mother praise !
The glory and the loveliness and might
Of Her Pure Womanly was made delight.

8

In that delight we rested, there to taste
   The fare of king Fidelius : being brought
To a round table, one named "Neverwaste,"
   A chaplain of the court, good joy besought,
And we were feasted on such royal cheer
As poets find, greeting the Lord's new year.

LXXVII.

1

Fraud hounds upon the track of miracle.
   Sincerity is chased by simulation.
Genius, conceiving of the Beautiful,
   Is mimicked by the fraudful imitation.
Fiction through all the winds of faith finds flight.
Wrong wrongs, in fatuous images of Right.

2

The antichrists rise in the path of Christ.
   The dragon's jaws close on the Golden Child.
Where Inspiration knew and improvised,
   Cold Calculation hammered, smoothed and filed,
To shape false images of God, and space
Falsehood's imposture in the holy place.

3

Betrayers, robed as angels of the light,
   Prove thus deceivers of the Word's elect ;
So the plumed satans urge a devious flight ;
   So pretence mirrors on from sect to sect.
So the endeared Society of Friends
In Orthodox and Hicksite seeming ends.

4

Spake king Fidelius, breathing to mine ear,
  "A seed of God remains in Mammon's seat.
There are two caverns and a single fear:
  Through them faint echoes of the Word repeat,
As sounds from mountains, creeping through the dales,
Whelmed in reverberation that prevails.

5

"Could I but clothe in mine old leathern skin,
  And, speaking as the Spirit moves, affirm,
Ears would withdraw, as from a speech of sin,
  And flying dove would seem a stinging worm.
By times, forms, tongues and customs fall apart,
As drop the petals when the germ takes heart.

6

"Against the steeple houses did I grieve?
  Here in the heaven of Friends cathedrals show,
And godly bishops to the rites achieve
  That terrified my simple mind below.
As when the royal sun for day comes forth,
Robed in red gold and purple o'er the earth,

7

"Thus priests on Lady's day pontificate,
  While on the other days they make good cheer:
The holy eucharist they celebrate,
  For the transubstantiations, that endear
God to the people, as the bread and wine
Upon the common board hold worths divine.

8

"So there are singing women, singing men,
   And those who play upon the keys and strings.
The inner light is outer lightened, when
   The Word-song fills the common worshipings.
Great are our joys, but richly they increase,
When life to its full ritual finds release.

9

"Five days there are for us in place of seven :
   The first is Lord's day ; then our mights are first ;
New forces to great industries are given ;
   New inspirations flow, divinely nursed.
The realm, as ever by conceptual plan,
Stands in Christ's Manhood as the working man.

10

"The last day of our week is Lady's day :
   'Tis then the realm postures in love's repose.
The Bride, the Spouse, the Mother in display
   Withdraws us to the stillness, to disclose
Beauties of holiness from bride to bride :
Face to Her face the land is glorified.

11

"'Tis all in Christ; all in the inner light;
   Old self abolished; serpent lost in dove.
Friends unto friends to common ends unite;
   The wisest of the land bear rule whereof
Their special gifts may testify ; so all
Dwell in one equity ; so none in thrall.

12

" Doth it not strike thee, Christ was a great Player,
  Player and Playwright both? He touched the sense,
And, touching it, opposed mankind's betrayer:
  The human drama is His evidence.
Temple and stage in one shall Him declare,
And common spectacle hold common prayer.

13

"Into Mankind's career He leads His act.
  What if Lord Christ and Lady figure yet;
Arch Lover and Arch Loveress redact,
  And so transpose Romeo and Juliet?
What if time's curtain lifts, to show the scene;
Shakspeare transcended by the Nazarene?

14

"Lord Christ sails in time's barge on galilee;
  Round Him all mortal passions whirl in storm;
All waves of thought heave to one troubled sea.
  What if the waters feel His moving form?
What if the whirling passions rest, to fill
With loving God-life for His 'peace be still'?"

15

I sat with queen Fidelia afterward,
  Saying 'the good king is right eloquent.'
"He is in a concern; in a regard;
  His righteousness leans to the earth's event."
So spake she; "when he sleeps, I hear him sing,
'Comfort my people, Comfort, comforting.'"

LXXVIII.

1

Ego, its mental strain is pugilistic ;
  Its final argument the killing blow :
Its common sense turns on the kindly mystic,
  His deeds all airs of peace in balmy flow.
"What will you do about it ?" answered he
To outraged Right, the chief of Tammany.

2

That Peace would triumph, overcoming War,
  Such truth friend Fox witnessed for Christendom.
Peace o'er time's forehead leads her morning star :
  The Friend is coming, Friendship is our home.
The Friendly People, from their heaven anigh,
Breathe to mankind by fluent melody.

3

Sooth, we to foes the other cheek have turned ;
  We for the Word in fourthness who declare.
Our hearts within to holy fire have burned ;
  Our bosoms pulsed God's breath to outer air.
Sundry have wrought to outrage and betray ;
Robbed, slandered, smitten ; they have had their way.

4

Keeping God's peace through all of this, we toil
  On, ever onward, to the peaceful end.
Heaven opens to us through such fierce turmoil ;
  So by full friendliness we meet the Friend.—
A Lady beautiful in summer bloom
Beamed on me ; thus rose Christa from the tomb.
  11

5

Spake She, as speech may be interpreted
  Through the part language of the partial third,
"Into earth's thirdness was My person led,
  Being in-worded in the Bridal Word.
Now as that Woman Yessa, for your sake,
I manifest, as when We rose to take,

6

"Twain-one, the earthly resurrection on.
  Then Jesus, as ye know, was outwarded.
The former time had from Our vision gone,
  And We beheld in future time instead;
Seeing this time-world, as it soon must be,
Folded within Us to eternity.

7

"So, after forty days, We drew our feet
  Into the path of the ascensive powers.—
Rise with Me into Lilistan; repeat
  My thoughts within you, as by falling flowers
That fold to speech by music of sweet verse.
Thus in the song thy bosom I immerse.

8

"Sprinkled thou wert with the baptismal water:
  Now I baptize thee in the vocal flame;
Leading in twain-one flesh the spousal daughter,
  Dear to thee ever by her four-fold name.
The concept of the Word by four-fold plan
Germed in ye; now 'tis heavened in Lilistan.

9

"Yea, 'blessed are the twain-one,' saith the Spirit;
  'For they inhabit peace.'   Arise and see.
In thy Lord's righteousness thou dost inherit
  Thy Lady's holiness, twain-one, full free.
The peace that passeth understanding flows,
All nuptial-wise, through wakening and repose.

10

"Time holds a claim upon Us, time and space,
  So far as human hearts are there to quicken.
Our twain-one heart enlarges, to embrace
  All who for godness yearn, though spoiled and stricken.
More offspring and more Father-Mother still!
Heaven grows as kingdoms in it shape and fill.

11

"Into the earthly youthness We were shapen,
  A twain-one God-Babe; so our fruited gold
Entered the planet's womb; thus to awaken,
  Wrapped for such time-birth in the fleshly mould.
Circling through orb to orb from sun to sun,
Our rounds of visual incarnations run.

12

"I touch the clarion in thine ear, to ring
  With fluent melodies of living sound;
Thy bosomed lyre I thrill impassioning.
  Awake thee to the Bridal Word unbound;
I dissipate the winters from thy shell;
I rise therein, the Woman of the well.

13

"The ever changeful universe of things
   May by a seeming from its form withdraw;
But thence to sight a new creation springs;
   The ever new infiniverse of law.
Things change; thoughts ever from Us, Twain-One, pass
To heavens that mirror in time's pictured glass.

14

"When thou wert but a simple, psychic thing,
   A glowing sprite as imaged ariel,
My bosom held thee; breathed thee forth, to wing
   By mystic, myriad ways to Annie's bell.
Thy twain-one home is in My house of glee;
Thy spaceness opened in Infinity.

15

"Scant not thy thought for time's misunderstanding.
   Scant not the pressure of the will to live.
Fear not the futures that await their banding.
   Cling to the lips divine that utterance give.
Ope to the current that holds God in flow.
Art thou bestowed upon? 'tis to bestow.

16

"A thought, a thought, a thought and yet a thought;
   'Tis thus four-folded man is built upon;
The simplist mind into its concept wrought;
   The life-notes marshaled to their unison;
The harmony of being in its will
Concentered; so My words to thee fulfill.

17

"As when heaven's river finds its cataract,
   Yet leaps not to the downfall but the rise,
So, by the confluent force in vital act,
   Led to new course through landscapes of the skies,
Life may the burden of its current bear,
To lift, full heavened, in weightlessness from care.

18

"So may a man glide over that which seems,
   In THAT-WHICH-Is to be forever blest;
So enter where the doing well supremes;
   Labor in labor led by rest in rest.
Touch to the nerve where most My doings play;
Touch to the Holiest for thy staff and stay."

LXXIX.

1

The Mother known in Jeremiah's phrase,
   "She who is hidden in the name of Yod."
The Ancient folds the Ancientess of days,
   "The Gladness of the gladnesses of God."
Airs, waters, fragrant earth, melodious flame
Reveal Her to us by the Four-fold Name.

2

I glimpsed a Sleeping Beauty, in the wood
   Where king Fidelius holds a pleasure seat.
Passing I touched in meditative mood,
   A solar lion watchful at her feet.
Joyous in bosom for the lovely sight,
I trode the wood path lifted by delight.

3

The king, now in a rest from cares of state,
    All as a yeoman, tiller of the soil,
Made beckoning, beaming from a brow elate,
    Holding the blessing of repose from toil.
Sweet is the pastime, exquisite the mirth
We taste, in touch with aromatic earth.

4

Here talked we afterward in priestliness.
    The holy book grew forth upon his knee;
The "volume of Ten Thousand Witnesses,"
    A Word-scroll textured through his memory.
The vital facts to verbal imprint grow,
By fourthness through the man unfolded so.

5

"Thus Shakspeare, Dante, Plato thought," he spake;
    Their glowing effigies the pages bore.
The real likenesses of manhood take
    Form, color, light, illustrating the lore.
Seen through each countenance, a lovely grace
Beamed to us; each revealed the Mother's face.

6

"The inner sense is that which to us lives";
    Spake he again; "a cup may hold the sea.
Scriptured, pictorial, through the four-fold sieves,
    Drop the gold sands of truth in melody.
The Man is in the book, as here we scan
How that the volume may be born of man.

7

"'Of the ten Sephiroth,' the magi said,—
  'The All-Creating and the All-Commanding,—
Are two, God-Man God-Woman interwed:
  Chokmah is Wisdom, Binah Understanding.
Chokmah begets, Binah conceives thereof
Truthness from Truth and lovingness from Love.'

8

"So God begets in timeness for a time;
  Goddess conceives in spaceness for a space.
But time and space as one-in-twain incline,
  Ingenerating shadow by embrace.
Thus told a poet of the God Most High,
'Nature is shadow that we see Him by.'

9

"Hear thence a lesson of the Archimage:
  This is our Word; Eternal Daughter-Son.
Chokmah in Binah are His heritage;
  The Well-Belovéd Aye-Proceeding One,
Who is above all things, before them all;
The Tree of Life, Arch-Eden, Way and Wall.

10

"Word was in the beginning; Word was God.
  Word was with God, the Light before the shade;
The Word concealed within the name of Yod,
  By whom all things from archetypes were made.
Here Israel ended; closed the lettered mesh.
Seer-prophets knew and waited Word made flesh.

11

" Passing the thought of third dimensioned mind,
    Surpassing feel of correlated sense,
Such wisdom by the greek was undivined,
    And to the hebrew vailed, obscure and dense.
By the unworded mind 'tis counted vain ;
'Tis the Word in us that the Word makes plain.

12

"So the True Light the world of mind was in,
    And the unworded world received Him not ;
Yet those, from ego who the mind could win,
    Beheld the Lamb of God, withouten spot
Or blemish or the shade of evil thing ; —
God, made Man Innocence and witnessing."

13

Ended he here ; led to his garden house.
    The Sleeping Beauty, now the servitress,
Gave toothsome viands ; her blithe, beaming spouse
    Invoked God Righteousness-in-Holiness.
Grand was his bearing, reverent, worshiping,
Bowed to the Joyous Queen in Joyful King !

14

So, whilst we fed with hearty appetites,
    Fidelia, habited as kitchen queen,
Broke warbling to a song of summer nights ;
    Touching her breasts by interludes between,
Till from them rose to sight, by rounding swells,
Song-billows ; taking shape as flowery dells,

15

Gay woodlands, flying gardens in the air,
   Filled with the joy of love birds caroling;
The Mother Moon, a Lady with gold hair,
   Ascendant, compassed by a four-fold ring
Of bright star maidens: so the vision passed
Into a sea of odor, sweetest last.

16

Hence, being fed, the king drew to his knee
   A white page; writ in letters violet gold;
So in his correspondence made to see.
   Scroll after scroll was preciously unrolled,
But thence Fidelia slipped them from his knees;
Twined them in air-shapes, wingéd for the breeze,

17

And tossed them to the flight with joyous laughter;
   His royal words to kinsmen of the land.
Who would not yearn for such divine Hereafter?
   But now the queen arose; I kissed her hand
With reverence, more than reverence: one, mine own,
Out-leaning touched her lips.— I stood alone,

18

A silent, solitary man. Returned
   Soon after to my earth-place I indite.
The joy that lives, within my bosom urned,
   Stirs to the memory of such dear delight;
So now I muse, the flowing lines between,
Of king Fidelius and his household queen.

PART FOURTH

"Behold, the tabernacle of God is with men, and He will
dwell with them, and they shall be His People, and He shall
be their God.   And God shall wipe away all tears from their
eyes ; and there shall be no more death, neither sorrow nor
crying, neither shall there be any more pain : for the former
things are passed away."

REV. XXI. 3, 4.

CONVERSATION IN HEAVEN.

LXXX.

1

Man is immortal, in true acceptation,
  By imputation of God's worded life;
This made his own through an assimilation,
  In simple sweet heroic patient strife,
To serve the good in all things, good in true.
This the New Life, the life forever new.

2

This is eternal life; to feel and know
  The Lord, the Word made flesh, our ground of hope,
Our substance of existence, and to grow
  Into His likeness-image, till the scope
Of hope and fear is lost in certainties;
The Word our light; His Form our paradise.

3

Only as God stands in him man is man;
  Yet God is in him by an imputation,
To will, to work, to meditate, to plan.
  But man unmakes himself by desecration;
Shell after shell, mind, spirit, soul are lost
In vacuo; germs that perish for dull frost.

4

Mere seeming man must end in dissolution;
"Dust that he is, to dust he shall return."
Death is his stand-place; death the path's conclusion;
First fails his outer shell, a broken urn.
The lives reluct, the senses make demur,
They shrink instinctive from the sepulcher.

5

The shell that is man's memory-form, his geist,
Is hence his outermost; time's dim frontier,
Its border-land, thence to the sense apprised:
There he in new-wrought seemings holds the year;
The solar world unseen save by its gleams;
Its image, by a ghostliness that streams

6

Through the stained windows of the earth's mankind.
A world of shades below the space we press,
As hades or elysium 'twas divined,
Part imaged in the grecian consciousness.
The seeming man led there, a mortal yet;
Led vaguely from remembrance to forget.

7

This is the world whereto the Roman thought
To find the spectral manes of his dead.
'Tis here the Hebrew for a rest besought;
The under-world where shades are quieted;
Where there is no new knowledge, nor device,
Nor growth of pains, nor spoil for avarice.

8

So posed it to the earthly bards and seers;
But to those dwelling in it not the same;
The unspent motions of their natured years
Surviving in a shadowed nature game.
Earth has its ages, iron, bronze or stone;
There the same ages, but as shadows known.

9

The gandaveer, larve, spectre, spook and ghost,
"Gorgons and horrors and chimeras dire,"
Were imaged shapes, projected o'er the coast
Of human fear or fancy or desire;
Wraiths in the moving mirage, floating far,
Glimpsed on the vague horizon's shadowed bar.

10

All that Earth fashioned stood again in Hades,
But by a wasting semblance, growing less;
The hierarchs and kings, the knights and ladies,
Deceased to dwell in other-worldliness;
Made sensitives, made psychics, mediums all
For an illusive custom past recall;

11

Not spiritual, but a "spiritism";
Never inspired, but "inspirational";
Their minds a vacuo in magnetism;
Earthly mankind their house of food and call;
"Revisiting the glimpses of the moon";
Oft dreaming of "re-incarnation" soon.

12

Sects, pastimes, customs there in wan survival ;
    Frolic, sport, farce or tragedy grown stale ;
Yet shaping feebly to a new arrival ;
    Failing and varying as an oft-told tale ;
Earth's marriage ways renewed, in vacuo spread ;
Feast of cold gods, the banquet of the dead.

13

Here Brutus toils anew the blade to grasp,
    And bring proud Julius gasping to the knee.
Here Cleopatra finds again her asp,
    As real as the shade of Antony.
Here the robed augur from the altar hales
The victim to inspect the sanguine trails.

14

'Twas all a death, in outlet from a dying ;
    Changeful mock-vision of a gradual swoon ;
Not an ascension but a deep down-lying ;
    The mortal insect in more frail cocoon,
Shaped as the old one cleft its failing shell ;—
A pseudo evolution nigh to hell.

15

So the old Faiths impinged upon the facts ;
    Broken, distorted, wrought by priestly arts
For superstition's drama, that enacts
    By many spectacles to fill the marts
Of third dimensioned custom, and to round
Time's orbit in a spectral wonder-ground.

LXXXI.

1

"Space is the unadorned vacuity,
   And time a motion through its linears led ;
A space of sea, where yet there is no sea ;
   A space of soil, where soil not yet dispread ;
A space of air, where air is not yet born.—
Breaths enter, of creations to forewarn.

2

" The breath of God creates the universe ;
   'Tis the first witness of the Archimage.
The potencies, in odors that immerse,
   To the etheric cloud for floods empage.
Creation lives, an orb of flowing seas,
Breaking to globules for the galaxies.

3

"God breathes for joy into the living sea,
   And so the flood respires; the fluid suns
Thrill to the universal harmony.—
   'Tis thus the story of creation runs."
The Ancient held his knees impact to mine ;
Grew forth the God-book : how the pages shine !

4

But thence I felt the knees thrill masterly.
   "Yea," spake he, "feel the motion ; it is time."
The motion grew, through instep, feet to ply ;
   Their nerves received a palpitating rhyme.
"Time shapes in rhythms; times in times achord.
Enter, through time, eternity, its Lord.
   12

5

"Man must be born in time, that hence he may
  Enter eternity as born again.
The fourth dimension through the third makes play
  That mortals may be wrought immortal men."
Like iron at last the vigors grew to feel ;
Made solid basic force that met the heel.

6

Achilles was invulnerable, all
  Save in the heel ; this only failed to be
Immersed, as grecian poesies recall,
  In bath of fluent immortality.
Forth from the storied past, the ancients drew
Mythes, that involved the truths wherefrom they grew.

7

The serpent Ego, the edenic snake,—
  The "woman's seed shall crush his venomed head,"
So God to Adam in the garden spake,
  "But he shall bruise the heel"; 'tis there intread
The arrears of the powers, that oppose
Man, who would to eternity unclose.

8

We saw how Christa pressed Her heel upon
  Earth's ignominies: that which smites on us
In these last years, almost through time agone,
  Is warfare of the ignominious.
The sympathies stand in one human shape ;
So by the heel they crush upon the snake.

9

He stings them, where they meet him to efface
  Selfdom in the unselfness : 'tis the last
Of the deliria that infest the race.
  Passing the arrear foe all foes are passed ;
The feet leave ignominy, for the rise
To the pure light where God is paradise.

10

Make thou no answer to the enmities ;
  But hold to crush the head of ego's worm.
Hold till God in thee by a timeness plies,
  To make thy tread as iron to the term.
When the last wounds that in the heel make plight
Are closed, Achilles, thou hast won the fight.

11

In such grave silence did the Master tread,
  On, on to Calvary ; through death trode He ;
At each pained step He met the Serpent's head.
  Such is our four-fold path to victory.
Still follow, follow, till the iron heel
Shapes in a body wrought as vital steel.

LXXXII.

1

I met a Roman, the centurion
  Who saw Christ crucified and pitied Him.
The tender soul through all these years has gone,
  Still feeling, in Christ's pity led to swim.
The Pitying Martyr caught his pity so,
Meeting its touch by love in overflow.

2

The iron warrior made a mental stroke,
　　As thus my feet in Christ to hold: a bliss
Of healing kindness thrilled me till it spoke;
　　He breathed warm pity, as by lips to kiss;
He touched mine eyes by reverence, to repeat
Joy, serving thus God's pity to the feet.

3

A quaker lady named Elizabeth
　　Said, "unto George this dear centurion came,
As bearing precious oils from Nazareth.
　　He witnessed on to others by the same;
So, where Friend's charities to service burn,
As ministering friend he holds concern."

LXXXIII.

1

The dew of Christ is as no other dew;
　　'Tis love in impregnation; on the rose
Of womanhood it falls; it trickles through
　　Her being, multiplying to the close;
It flows to waters, sprinkles by sweet rains,
Quenches the fires that riot in the veins.

2

Spake Annie, solemn, slow, "thou, thou beloved,
　　Whom I did bear, 'twas mother milk divine,
The dew of Christ, that in my body moved,
　　Baptizing thee; warm blood of Christ the vine.
So thou art as a grape on Christ the Bough,
Made multiplying clusters until now."

3

She vanished, vanished in a mist of tears,
  The halo of Christ's pity; but anon
I felt, as feeling through the cloud of years,
  Remembrance of a sacred hour bygone,
When Annie, as an angel, o'er my bed
Shone witnessing; such word as this she said:

4

"My child, poor child, always of this remember;
  God is your Father, and your brother man."
'Twas in a night of youth's most drear December,
  Wounded, athirst; the pity broke, it ran
Through mists that goldened, till supernal day
Lit the dark room; December lost in May.

5

Thenceforth my life changed: touched by motherhood,
  The calyx of the soul wreathed lips to part:
The pure in beautiful, the true in good,
  The brave in conduct, lyrical in art
Rose in me as the vine may from its root;
Yea, and thereafter Christ was borne to fruit.

6

Time passes on, but Christ's heart throbs in time;
  Time grows, the heart-beats thrill with mightier force;
Time heightens, Christ uplifts through it sublime;
  Time deepens, Christ is made its rivered course;
Time culminates, 'tis then Lord Christ we see;
We enter Him, Christ is Eternity.

LXXXIV.

1

"Creations rise in breathings of the Word.
　The universe is led, a living song,
Octaves from octaves, universal chord,
　Sounds upon sounds: the sweet harmonic throng
Guide, through impassioned flowings of the fire,
Swift wingéd shapes, the soul-germs of desire.

2

" Creation so is God's desire in motion ;
　Desires, desires, the ever-flowing sea ;
God-life in germ-lives heaving to their ocean ;
　Word-song in universal melody ;
Life, swept along in billows of glad sound ;
Desires, led through desires by vorticed round.

3

"Fire, water, air and aromatic earth,
　In the Divine Maternity, their bed,
To substance of persistence rhythm forth,
　Eternal, infinite ; the fountain-head
Wherein the word-desires by music flow,
As Word-flames in them for the sunbeams glow."

4

The Ancientess of days deliciously
　Spake, if such vibrating be speech by name,
"Song is perpetual bridal ecstasy
　In God One-Twain ; the word-desires outcame,
Born in the song to fold and co-exist ;—
The myriad joy-lives of the pleasure mist.

5

" Binah is understanding, overstanding ;
    Binah instanding and outstanding, four;
Pasts, presents, futures, finals knowing, wanding,
    Through time, Her motion, and through space, Her floor ;
Omega so in Alpha weaves Her dress ;—
The Mother Life whose Form is Loveliness.

6

" The Mother of creation 'tis who sings
    In the small fays that rhythm to thine ear ;
Such were the word-desires, whose carolings
    Wrought one melodious murmur, when the sphere
Of the arch-cosmos opened for the rod
Of impregnation ;—God in Woman God.

7

" Such word-desires dwelt in one knowingness,
    Instilling joy to joy in such sweet breath ;
Organic earths, airs, waters, flamenesses.—
    Binah, in Christus-Christa, 'tis who saith,
' Thou in thine inmost art a psychic ray ;
A word-desire, man fay to woman fay.'

8

" Return into thy fairy mind again ;
    By interstanding find the fairy floor."—
Lo! I was in-stanced with the little men ;
    A fairy parson met me at the door ;
Welcomed me to a fairy conclave hall ;
A palace in the brain-world, largely small.

LXXXV.

1

I sat at ease with one, the fairy Moses;
    That fay who was the word-desire of him
Who, as the lore of Israel discloses,
    Was once, a man-babe where the lilies brim
Upon the yellow bosom of old nile,
Drawn from his ark of rushes, for awhile

2

To find a refuge from the famished water,
    And taste sweet mother milk from woman's breast,
And stand affirmed by Egypt's princely daughter,
    Clad in rich honors as such themes attest;
And hence find entrance to the mysteries, known
In the dread halls where Isis orbs her throne.

3

Twelve fairies held in common care, as plighted
    Into twelve months that rule time's rounding year;
Fays who, in Egypt's hierophants, delighted
    To shape the knowings whence the truths appear;
And wisdoms to the outerstand enlarge;
And sensitives wreathe to the body's marge.

4

Graced in a rounded calm, the conclave smiled,—
    Grave infants who through rounding time had passed;
Spake, twelve-in-one, "time shall be unbeguiled."
    The fairy who found Moses, for the last,
Finished the phrase with, "time is all a-flow;
Earth shall be found, as Moses long ago.

5

"Out of his wicker basket on time's nile,
  Man shall uplift by the Great Lady's quest.
Mankind shall open its broad eyes to smile,
  Caught to the milky fountains of Her breast."
Lowly responded all the little men,
"Yea, yea, Her coming lifts mankind again."

LXXXVI.

1

Stately, in Egypt's carved and polished lore,
  Dwelt the man Moses when, from virgin youth,
He knelt the Holy Woman to adore,
  Whom magi sought and owned as Mother Truth.
He strove, with shadowed Isis to prevail;
He kissed her hem to serve and never fail.

2

Four aspects are whereby man Moses shows:
  His work is met in Israel's house of bone.
The wisdom of that service would unclose
  A little, through the fay-world faithly known.
He entered fourthness to its first degree;
That which reveals God Truth in unity;

3

That which is sculptured in the name of Yod,
  The Jehovistic concept from the Word.
Up to this height as Sinai he trod;
  By meekness of approach the Voice he heard.
By twain-one grace I met the very man,
High on the sacred mount of Lilistan.

4

His love was with him to that lady height.
   Upon his knees outgrew the holy book,—
Their knees together; a divine delight
   Flowed through it, in such wise the mountain shook,
And there were thunders that in music rolled,
And lightnings that enwove to curtained gold.

5

Then Issa came; she led four knees to meet.
   Through his right arm Moses the word-staff drew,
And in a voice, as when starred magi greet,
   By tones that thrilled the breathful bosom through,
Led by deep interbreathings into mine,
Spake of the mysteries that his days entwine.

6

Moses, in genius purely aryan,
   Was yet in flesh of the semitic wrought;
A very grecian by the worded plan,
   Shrewd as Ulysses, who, whilst heroes fought,
Toiled for the victory of arms in arts,
As Wisdom by the opportune imparts.

7

He was full deep, but in no base concealment.
   In secret ways of human nature versed,
He knew that time was rife for re-revealment
   Of God-lore by the token of the First.
He served Truth's opportune, to weave a spell
That should evolve a people, Israel.

8

He knew that to lead forth a cruel horde,—
    'Twas in such thought his wisdoming began,—
A people who must win their soil by sword,
    Truth must be imaged as the Mighty Man,
Jehovah of the hosts; hence to proclaim
The unity of God his task became.

9

He knew that in one people this must be
    Infashioned, wrought by miracle and sign,
To stand opposed to time's idolatry,
    Whereto had died the olden faiths divine.
He knew that to a people, hard of heart
And cruel to the core, he must impart

10

A current of sure energy, to hold
    Their abject selfishness, and serve the ends
Of the great purpose, that from ages old
    Works on, and to mankind's renewal tends.
He was a servant of the "hidden fire,"
And so shaped Israel for its rugged lyre.

11

Hence he excluded all things from the cult,
    That shadowed God the Masculine from view.
He swung his teaching as a catapult,
    To smite the fraudful adepts, who pursue
The paths where men to apparitions feel:
Upon the 'spiritist' he set his heel.

12

That faith in God as Personal would perish,—
    As it is perishing on earth to-day,—
Were this inchoate people free to cherish
    Fictioned theosophy, that held a sway
In magic conclaves, this he knew beside,
And closed the pit wherein old ages died.

13

"The secret things belong to God" he cried.
    As say the Friends, "for this he held concern."
He sought to build, to build, and to provide
    Against the inroads that shape overturn.
He knew that priests conserve, that ritual forms
A stronghold for the faith against the storms.

14

So he built Israel in conservatism.
    The pillar of the Truth he held erect,
A living rock, to breast the occult schism
    Of all encroaching evil, and protect
The worship of God One, its moral creed,
Though man should faint thereby and woman bleed.

15

Orbed in calm intellect, he traveled far
    By spiritual insight; was aware
He showed to Israel the rocky bar,
    Vailed the deep sea divine that crested there;
Yet questing on, he saw that One should rise
In Israel, of the mystery to apprise.

16

Holding his labors but provisional,
  He thought t'ward Israel of a latter day ;
Clasping in God the source and terminal ;
  Broadened through all the nations to array ;
Owning God Man, born in the flesh to bless
The world, its Righteousness in Holiness.

17

By hints, half spoken phrases, speech of looks,
  Kind manners, meeknesses, fraternal wiles,
He breathed a wisdom that no written books
  Could dare express.—A thunder on him piles ;
His brow is vailed in wisdoms darkly grand ;
Lightnings flame through him, worded staff in hand.

LXXXVII.

1

The knees were parted and the book invailed.
  Again I write : the mild September day
Hushes her airs to slumber.   I inhaled
  The Mother's balm, it rhythmed in the lay.
I taste the aster and the golden rod,
Mixed with the blossoms of the breath of God.

2

Through alien airs I force a distant speech ;
  The earthly world, enwrapt in shadows gray,
Shows but by mortal shells upon its beach ;
  Yet Wisdom meets them by the lyric spray ;
Life from the billows of the flowing sea,
Whose crested waves ope lips of melody.

3

"Our conversation is in heaven," Paul spake,
 "Whence also cometh Christ, our Expectation;
So these vile forms, wherein our spirits ache,
 Shall change unto His glorious conformation.
For this He is full able to pursue,
Making all things in His own likeness new."

4

'Tis in the faith of the Apostle's creed,
 The path of faith, Faith's witness, that I wing
Thought's that do burn in sympathies that bleed;
 I too a friend "concerned for witnessing."
Through Moses lined the Christ-faith unto Paul;
Christ-Christa is our all, our very all.

5

I memorized; no more I memorize,
 Save as the Word for pasts would so array;
My home is in the wedded sanctities.
 Bear with me yet a little, whilst I say
Peace, 'peace that passeth understanding' flows,
By interstanding, for the sure repose.

6

I caught to Christ lore, as the overbough
 That swings anigh pent swimmers in the stroom,
When nearing cataracts their might avow,
 And whirling mist-wreaths darken for the doom.
Christ was the Bough, the Tree; His grace upbore.
Find home-rest in Him, love, believe, adore.

LXXXVIII.

1

"Calm night," said Plato, "night that breedeth thought."
    There is a darkness that enfolds the day,
The Mother Darkness: through starred silence wrought,
    A mystery of Truth I hence assay.
He that hath ears that breathe a voice may hear,
That moves in rhythms; dewy flames appear;

2

They touch the nostrils for discrimination.
    The mystery of sex in perfume hides,
Through immanation drawn to emanation.
    The violet odor breathes of wedded brides;
Rose led through violet full wifely bloom.
Life's odor sea is hived in Christa's womb.

3

Johannes writ of "vials full of odor";
    Inhaled them so; "these are the prayers of saints."
The Wife stood nigh me; fragrance overflowed Her.
    Spake She, "We shrine such wives; 'gainst fears and faints.
The breaths of God in woman overbrim,
Meeting the sense of man to hearten him.

4

"'Tis the enwomaned man who leads advance
    In faiths and cultures; fashions for the charts
Of new discoveries; opens the romance;
    Creates the poesies; renews the arts.
But that Minerva's bosom charmed her son,
Never had shone Athena's parthenon.

5

"Opes through the nostrils of the worded man
   The Woman's Word, breathes for him purely sweet.
Minds that the truth-wave flowed are coldly wan,
   Till they are billowed in Her bridal heat."
She smiled; I kissed the grace-ring on Her hand.
Lo! 'twas the Queen, the Lady of God's land.

6

All night, as one awake in Jacob's tent,
   I wrestled with the Mother of sweet fires;
Till, won to Her by a divine consent,
   Rest found me in the concord of Her lyres.
Then mine enworded eyes beheld the glades,
Blest by the myriads of Her white robed maids.

7

Rare fragrance of the Mother's holiness
   Robes them enlilied, haloes breast and brow:
Thus the ten thousand thousand witnesses,
   Her "vials of sweet odors," there avow.
"Prayers of all saints" enfill them, they exhale,
They breast, they breathe, they wrestle and prevail.

8

One touched me in the nerve of supplication;
   But hence the nerve, in righteousness of might,
Drew ardencies that lead prolification
   Of song from song, from holiness delight;
Yet to the nostrils fed a pleasant smell
Of living odor from the Mother's well.

9

Tho round white girl was with me afterward,
  A wifely presence dipped to overbough.
Touched to the nostrils by a wise regard,
  A sapience grew that finds expression now.
The scent of prey that hawk or vulture shows
Is in the beak, fore-type of Israel's nose.

10

All sweets, by one pure odor of the good,
  Flow in the uprise and return of prayer;
But the glad fragrance to aromal food
  Grows in the wifeness of the nuptial pair.
The rounded grace breathed to a bridal kiss;
Left on the lips rich bread; prayers form to this.

11

"Man did eat angel's food." There was a labor
  In recent time that I was called to do;
It spake for sharpness as a mental saber,
  A sapience, guilt and guile to fathom through.
In prayerful rest, ere to such combat led,
My lips held transubstantiated bread.

12

Yea, 'tis explicit; bread grew in my lips;
  Grew such as loaves, work of the baker's art,
Cut for the bride cake, ere the wedded slip
  Away and for the honeymoon depart.
"Jest not with holy things."—I dare not jest;
Surely the bread was there, it left a zest
  13

13

That lingered, and the perfume filled the chamber,
   Lived all the night and all the coming day.
A godly widow, as she will remember,
   Made visit, and a morsel found its way
Into her mouth ; praising the Lord, she ate,
Inhaled warm fragrance richly delicate.

14

I say not, if the manna was a mythe,
   Or a descent of bread on Israel ;
Truths in old scripture to their symbols wive ;
   Yet bread from Worded lips may grow full well.
In miracle the years to years achord ;
We tell it not, our secret with the Lord.

15

These are the secrets of Truth's nuptial bowers.
   We hive them in the sanctuaried cell,
Curtained as in the ark, till some wise hour
   Breathes on the lips that poesies may tell.
"Man did eat angel's food" ; yea, now partake
Visioned or vailed, that sapience may awake.

LXXXIX.

1

That which man lacketh is discrimination.
   The third dimensioned egoists pursue
The processes of occult rumination,
   Till fiction forms its miracle to view.
The serpent rods, that Egypt's adepts plied,
Strove with the rod of Moses, but they died.

2

The danger from true miracle is this,
  That it arouses occult enmities.
The under world is troubled then to hiss;
  The phantoms are disquieted; they rise
Upon the Worded man to overwhelm,
Seeing he meets Event and grasps the helm.

3

The danger from true miracle beside,
  Is that the Worded man is classed with knaves
Who in the saddle, superstition, ride,
  And by its whip and bridle rule the slaves;
The fearful, credulous, oft kindly folk,
Who heed the crank as if an angel spoke.

4

Save us from cranks; Good Lord, deliver us
  From the small fry of fictioned men, the dupes
Of ego's fantasies; pestiferous,
  Malodorous in wastage of the "spooks."
Celestial orbs, the universe that gem,
'Tis not for ghost-play God created them.

5

An apt, learned jurist spake the other day
  Of Jesus, as a "thaumaturgic man";   .
Meaning a crank, fooled in the nature play,
  Thence fooling history for the Christian plan.—
My lady opened large and serious eyes,
Spake, "Christ to Israel seemed as such despise;

6

"A youth whom satan spawned and harlot bred.
   Their 'Toldoth Jesu' says his arts assailed
To pilfer from the temple's ark, and tread
   The holy place of holies, barred and vailed.
He stole the secret of the Master's word,
That ruled the rebel genii when they heard,

7

"And by it sought Jehovah to dethrone,
   And chain perverted Israel to his knees;
But upright Judas, true and valiant known,
   Despoiled him of his might of sorceries.
His vassals stole the body from the grave.—
'Tis 'hail Iscariot! born Jah's flock to save.'"

XC.

1

The "harp of Erin" is an occult fact,
   In fourth dimensioned rhythm; 'tis a man,
Holding full purpose to a Wordful act.
   Emmet, Wolfe Tone, ten others, they began
'Neath the green banner, whilst the anthem rolled
In solemn, sweet harp thunders, blithely bold.

2

The passion of a nationality
   Diffuses through the Irish Kelt; meanwhile
The World Soul vibrates to a surface ply,
   Grasping the people's foot-hold to their isle.
Man-woman Ireland toils, to shape in space
A rounding circle for a nation's place.

3

Saint Patrick, Saint Bridgida, two like these
   Held occult union in their blessed lives;
Toiling, as cloistered, sexless honey bees,
   To store the Christ-bread in monastic hives.
The fertilizing pollen of the grace
Of God was nurture to a famished race.

4

But such two wrought into a dear regard
   For each in other, and their wedded hearts,
When they had grown the thirdness to discard,
   Knit them, in-worded, wedded counterparts.
Patricius holds beneath the bannered green,
Arch-Ireland's king, one with the spousal queen.

5

A Christed Erin by such service grew.
   We view an Emerald Isle from Lilistan,
Bathed in perpetual verdure o'er the blue
   Sea waters: flutters there Her airy fan;
The Mother of the morn a breath bestows,
Blent in pure ethers to the violet-rose.

6

Etheric rivers tremble to the sea;
   All eloquent as speech they touch the strands;
The surges lip to kiss-waves joyously;
   The warm sweet billows meet like lovers' hands,
In holy troth-plight to each other lent,
Affirming dear chaste ardors of consent.

7

A city rises in a vast quadrangle,
  Circled by spiral avenues of groves
And pleasure seats; celestial stars bespangle.
  There Patrick dwells; delightsomely he moves,
Serving the realm; his palace, as 'twas shown,
Holds garden squares 'neath one great worship-dome.

XCI.

1

I was a guest one balmy afternoon;
  Patricius there, Patricia at his knee.
Through waning day kissed down the Lady Moon,
  Postured for coming dew-fall motherly.
So there these lovers, chastely delicate,
Drew to sweet converse from the cares of state.

2

Four knees drew nigh in worship; so, between,
  God's concept book for Erin rose to show.
As the white swans upon the billows preen,
  Mid playful cygnets goldenly aglow,
Patrick and queen Patricia met the sight,
Plumed o'er the flowings of the realm's delight.

3

But Patrick kissed Patricia, so to open
  The volume; then to sight the page grew clear
By water symbols, as when ice is broken
  And crystal wavelets touched by stars appear.
'Twas thus the flowing truths fed to the brain;
The nostrils opened, they respired amain.

4

The odor that is named "sanctification"
   Rose through Patricia's breast with balmy sighs;
But Father Patrick lifted adoration,
   Touching the sense where inspiration plies:
Then to a sapience our minds were knit;
We saw Earth's Erin by the skill of it;

5

Read by an overstanding its ideal;
   Saw of its kingdom climbing to declare,
A realm all royal, priestly, hymeneal,
   Waiting the inbreath of God's nuptial air;
A Church in State, a Theosocial whirl,
Toned in such order as the stars unfurl.

6

As the whorled bulb hid in the gardener's earth,
   Erin is now; the bulb must thrill and waken;
The lily by sure-foot stalk lift its worth,
   Then ope to living bloom by gladness shaken.
Freed from the vestiges of mortal shame,
"Saint Mary of the Isles" shall be her name.

7

I touch the hand of Her who mothers me;
   I bless the soil Her regal sandals meet.
Sweet hopes reach forth for Erin's destiny,
   As violet buds that part by vernal heat.
For Erin's fate I held a deep concern;
Patrick's, Patricia's hand so clasped in turn.

8

The volume closed its leaves of treasured bliss;
   Patrick kissed on my brow, the cross to sign.—
When blessed Mary, as young Artemis,
   Trips in the Word-truth o'er the breathing line;
Then as the virgin mother beams, and lifts
The Word Child on her breast for royal gifts;

9

The Isle that bears her name shall bloom, delivered
   Into the freedom of Christ's Holy See;
Shall glow, in Heavenly Hymen's grace transfigured,
   All royal, robed in twain-one liberty.
Thrill harp of Erin, thrill to Patrick's hand;
Thrill to the birth-rise of Saint Mary's land.

XCII.

1

Into Calamity I find the way.
   'Tis in calamity that earth-time hovers;
A fragile wreath of ceremonial spray;
   A grimy avalanche, mankind that covers;
A rush of incoherences; a strife,
That by its form deforms the human life.

2

Time-rot in mind-rot, time is led to grovel
   In the gross element where men decay.
Scholars construct their theoretic hovel
   From the grand ruins of an earlier day.
Great history, a lost scripture disinterred,
Holds, unawares to men, Earth's primal Word.

3

That Word in history is buried deep ;
   A vanished realm in ooze beneath the sea ;
Palace and shrine in broken shards, that heap
   O'er all that held divine antiquity.
Not isled atlantis, 'neath the surges curled ;
There the atlantean orb, man's primal world.

4

The tree of ages sheds its withered leaves,
   And the leaves moulder restfully and mute.
The faded past from memory bereaves,
   But the tree towers aloft in golden fruit.
All the rich God-growths of the aions old
Shape, in calamity their forms to fold.

5

For in calamity time's Judgment stands ;
   The Wondrous Woman robed in cloud and storm.
Her fingers ply amid the sundering strands,
   And through them show pale glimmerings of Her form.
Feel through calamity, full free to dare ;
Touch to the quick ; 'tis Judgment meets thee there.

6

Time's "pent up Utica contracts our powers."
   Calamity, that tracks the planet's round,
With feet in fire and brow in cloud that lowers,
   Weakens Earth's custom on its holding ground.
Each impress of those eager, flying feet
Stamps out some step-stone of the obsolete.

7

'Tis the humanity in man that waits.
  The common ego in mankind resists.
Calamity brings pressure, operates
  To serve the nobler manhood that persists.
Fold the frail infants in the cradles warm,
But trust young courage to the pelting storm.

8

It threads the level of the standing place,
  Whereon men by their masses crowd and coil:
Lifts here a barrier, opens there a space
  Abysmal; speeds the vantages to spoil;
Whirls a vibration through the ranks: they reel
And rend apart: so time is in repeal.

9

Time's moving form is now deformity.
  America, that rose, an affirmation
Of manhood's right, a proud enormity
  Becomes at last, a people's desolation.
Calamity, whose brow is in the cloud,
Weaves by her storm the dead time's burial shroud.

10

Interest and tax the harvest wealth consume.
  O'er the broad land the usurer is king.
Pandora's box no more, Pandora's womb
  For giant births of ill is opening.
Homes, hearths and altars graced the People's floor;
Floor is made quicksand, fails and is no more.

11

Ego-democracy, time's vainest cheat,
  Lifts, holds in place the rulership of knaves.
Ring into ring the bonds are forged complete ;
  Industrial cities crowd with clans of slaves.
Freedom, led captive through her lost domains,
In their proud capitol bleeds bound in chains.

12

Calamities that travail must converge.
  For this, thou sore-tried brother, have no fear ;
'Tis the full flood that leads the over surge,
  Reviving so the desert dry and drear.
Led through the "needful trouble of the rains,"
New life, heaven's life, shall find the thirsty plains.

XCIII.

1

I saw a martyr of the People, led
  Into a city of the four-fold wall ;
Good Lincoln ; there at first-time glance he said,
  "Great heaven! this beats the promise of Saint Paul."
Made welcome where the sacred throne-light shone,
He then exclaimed, "'tis Christ in Washington."

2

Upon a purple dais he was placed,
  O'ercome and dazzled by the splendor there.
The four-fold worship of the land embraced,
  Robed him in priestly surplice, and a pair
Of heavenly ministrants gave to his hand
A crozier, in a scepter and its wand.

3

He grasped it as a word-staff; but the mind
  Of his humility such phrase bespoke,
" Into an apple tree methought I climbed,
  And in a mighty robin's nest awoke
As a babe bird, but lay as if on pegs,
Fearing to stir lest should be broken eggs.

4

"But the eggs hatched, and out of them came four,
  That seemed to me young feathered cherubim,
Whose wings clasped round me, fluttered and upbore :
  Meanwhile a full, melodious people's hymn
Rose through them, caught me, filled me, whirled me far :
I broke through Washington ; now here we are."

5

One spake, "Son, here We are, and thou in Me.
  Behold the city, it is four-fold wide.
Open the mind of thy humility
  Into the mind of largeness I provide."
Then Lincoln saw, cried, in a grand relief,
"Christ, thou art God, the people's King and Chief."

6

'Twas in his land's calamity he wrought :
  Strove through it ; saw the day of peace uprear,
In shadows, to his apprehensive thought ;
  But then his own calamity drew near.
'Neath the assassin's blow, his bosom gave
Christ its last love ; 'twas thus he found the grave.

7

Priestly in kingliness, a People stands
    Orbed in that city of the four-fold wall.
Lincoln is cherished in the common hands,
    And feasted in their glorious banquet hall.
Four-fold the cherubs bore him wing in wing,
To serve that city as a priest and king.

XCIV.

1

'Tis pressure, pressure; everywhere 'tis pressure.
    Now the rich few, the life of God who steal,
And waste the years of men for vain self-pleasure,
    Foot as the dogs who serve to turn a wheel.
No man escapes, no woman; frost, that plies
Through autumn's night, wastes the gay butterflies.

2

The devotees of fashion are its drudges,
    The men of pastime and the men of prey;
Calamity the meager span begrudges;
    Fears haunt the hours that serve for holiday;
Wealth eats like poverty; hot blood, that drips
From heart-pierced Labor, stains the feasting lips.

3

Ever the pressure grinds, more fiercely cruel;
    Ever the competitions more intense.
The fire that climbs, with human lives for fuel,
    Sweeps through red flames to burials foul and dense.
Never so hard, since mortal time began,
For man to thrive yet be an upright man.

4

In the strained situation men are harried,
　　Like hares that race before the huntsman's pack.
Souls are opprest as Sindbad was who carried
　　The "old man of the sea" upon his back.
The long, lean, sinewy arms the neck entwine;
Men press ripe grapes, the beast fills with the wine.

5

Time hardens, and men's hearts by pressure harden,
　　Grow dense, grow callous to the common woe.
Once nature held a paradisal garden;
　　Now it holds hell on earth by overflow.
Street boys and girls, defiant, furtive, bold,
Show wizened faces, prematurely old.

6

Reverence for age is perishing from youth;
　　Mankind is verging to the fever stage;
Spectral illusions image for the truth;
　　The charlatan rules, trampling on the mage.
The eyeballs of mankind are seared; they spin
To a walpurgis dance their dreams within.

7

The universe a form of truth in reason;
　　The man a microcosm of its forms;
Shall this be so, and yet the Age of Treason
　　Reel on, nor fail, nor perish in the storms?
We stand in prison, in an iron room,
Whose walls contract to shape our living tomb.

8

Yet Judgment, moving on, is counter-pressure;
 She heaves full breasts to front the iron wall;
She nerves the Woman's will, its might to measure
 'Gainst the foul force that else o'ermasters all.
The fourthness breathes in battle with the third;
The Womanly of God has felt, has heard.

9

Break heart, thou heart; but open to the Sea.
 Sea of God's Womanly, thy floods awaken.
Through the last pressure may the Advent be;
 In the dread hour of bars let bars be braken.
We find the time-pulse faint, uncertain, slow,
And touch the moment of the Coming so.

XCV.

1

"Work while the day lasts, for night cometh soon,
 Wherein no man can labor"; 'tis a text
Phrased in the wisdom of the opportune.
 All that man doeth is to him annexed:
So it be wrought in rectitude, a ground
Is fashioned thus in the eternal round.

2

So Lincoln labored; an unselfness held,
 With God in purpose for a nation's life.
Never against his calling he rebelled:
 His time was buried in the worthful strife,
A people to revive and reinstate,
From the huge wreck where it lay desolate.

3

He held that God should be incorporate
    In public order, as in private worth;
His effort was mankind to elevate,
    That saints in fact should hence possess the earth.
Not much of saintliness he kept for show;
His to lift burdens of the common woe.

4.

"Infidel, Tyrant, Murderer, Buffoon,"
    Such the foul epithets hurled on his name.
He entered where the nation lay in swoon,
    Spell-bound, half-paralyzed by dread and shame.
The pathway broke to chasms where he trod;
Firm-footed he, his foot-faith held to God.

5

The tender hearted man, the just and fearless,
    The soul of love, the bosom free from guile:
For him the anxious nights were dry and cheerless;
    Days led through toil on toil as thunders pile;
The patient man, unflinching in his trust,
Held to God's ends by the divine "thou must."

6

From his shrewd eyes I caught a merry twinkle;
    Some happy jest was nigh his lips to tell;
His mouth was pursed, with laughter to besprinkle.
    Sitting at ease,—I knew the habit well,—
Quoth he, "decision, when it carries fate,
Makes it seem easy to the men who wait.

7

"Relax the mind first when you seek to brace it;
  Laughter holds courage, breeds a genial fire.
First realize the difficult, then face it,
  To fill with cheer the hosts you would inspire.
Colors at half-mast prophesy defeat;
Hold joyous valor to the topmost beat.

8

"Enough," spake he, "my coat is photographed,
  Yet here again the old coat is turned new.
The man who wept sat in the man who laughed;
  Seward nor Stanton saw the mantle through,
But Christ saw through; when labor seemed but loss,
My thought held to the Man upon the cross."

9

The sea-like swells of recollection ceased;
  A genial reverence suffused his face;
Thoughts to his present blessing-time released;
  Bearing grew stately, as became the place.
Into a priestly kingliness, he bore
The shrewd simplicity his earth time wore.

XCVI.

1

"Work while the day lasts"; look before from after.
  Here, where the larum bell from Sumpter tolled;
Where North and South clinched on the blazing rafter,
  As giants fight, whilst chaos 'neath them rolled;
I think unto the work of hearts in hands,
Where manifested God in Labor stands.

14

2

Judgment does not coerce, She liberates;
    Does not suppress but sets the motives free;
Uplifts in God the soul that supplicates;
    Enthrones the just in opportunity.
The New Jerusalem, from town to town,
Through blissful human labor settles down.

3

A spark of love loosens the cruel rigor,
    Wafts waves of sunshine through the quickening heart;
Then how much more shall Love Divine transfigure,
    Led on through counterpart to counterpart,
Borne on by thrills, the flesh that unprofane,
As human earth opes to the One-in-Twain.

4

"Labor is prayer"; the old monastic saying.
    Labor *sans* worship led through heart to hands,
Is but mock service, kin to a betraying.
    Labor is gladsomeness, that seas and lands
Rejoice for, when divine results are shown,
As rife fruitions, from their motives grown.

5

Say, "can the Ethiopian change his skin"?
    Yea, when the Word-life leads transcoloration.
The outer form as that which is within
    Reveals, when Word-sex grows to revelation.
So the starred night illumes to roseate morn,
And golden sunrise, through auroras born.

6

I sat with Lincoln in his private room;
  Mild respirations rose our breasts between.
Sudden he spake, " behold a rose in bloom!"
  A lady entered, priestess, muse and queen;
A dark, rich beauty, colored as ripe fruit;
Warm as by summer odor in pursuit.

7

"I saw the Lord," spake she, "our very Lord,
  Once, father Abram, as the Colored Man."
Her glorious bosom heaved, a grecian chord
  Thrilled through her voice, but that was african.
"Here I have seen His Lady; yes indeed,
The Lady of the Lord: we are their seed."

8

Sojourner Truth, called since "Deliverance";
  One who bore witness to the times at hand;
One who held firm in Freedom's long advance
  To blot the stains of bondage from the land,—
Then she was dark as tropic night, but now
The Mother's radiance robes her to the brow.

9

Here's an hereafter that is rich in gift;
  Its bosom heaves above our planet's line.
See how the transformations may uplift;
  Transcolorations tint to hues divine.
Twain continents, as day and night, embrace
In God, and race transfuses into race.

XCVII.

1

'Tis the transfusion of the life of Christ,
   Essential substance of the Nazarene,
That lifts man-woman, so imparadised,
   To image forth the Bridal King and Queen.
There's a young heaven that presses to the van
Of coming time, afro-american.

2

Survival of Word-purpose led through act;
   Survival of organic good in true;
Survival of the life-toil, held compact
   In the divine affections that pursue;
Survivals of beatitudes, reborn
From God through men toiling in times forlorn;

3

Survival of the Worded man, in that
   Which from the Word-life grew in deeds to be;
'Tis such that lifts an heavenly ararat,
   Mountain of God, in timed eternity.
It rises o'er the floods that clasp its base;
An infant eden folds in its embrace.

4

"Jacob kissed Rachel, lifted voice and wept,"
   His bosom cradled to a sweet repose;
Abram kissed Sojourner, whom God had clept,
   And Goddess blossomed through as Eden's rose.
By interpresence, God their beings drew
To interfusion, making all things new.

5

Such is conjugial union in the skies:
   No marriage there as is by worldlings known;
But wedded harmonies in melodies;
   Groom led through Christ's and Bride through Christa's
      throne.
"Married?" nay, not as mortal ego dreams;
But Christa-Christed, led to living streams.

6

Of men and women mightiest to serve,
   Through the fierce crisis-years that freed the slave;
What powers in confluence their Word-lives nerve!
   What firm results their sacred stand-place pave!
Freedom grew through them by the earth's pursuit;
But a new heaven in heaven is ripened fruit.

7

The fragrance of twain grand, good lives; that led
   Through balmy gifts of toil, floats there suspended;
Till a young atmosphere is in it bred,
   Holding rich Word-breath with its ethers blended.
So each new heaven breathes, in its local tide
Of atmosphere, fed by the Bridegroom-Bride.

8

'Tis Word-attraction weaves association.
   Beings, by sympathies most near akin,
Draw to a special thought and conversation;
   Styles, tastes, modes, habits, colors to the skin.
We are with those we love the most to meet,
In sympathies that rhythm, brow to feet.

9

Hence those "who many turn to righteousness"
    Shine there "as stars forever and forever,"
Concentered in a mightiness to bless,
    That "follows them," the fruit of life's endeavor.
Motives, in bosomed God that held their tryst,
As mights in timed eternity persist.

XCVIII.

1

A Nation comes that is not yet a nation,
    As Christ-Apollo born to sway the sphere;
In evolution 'tis divine creation.
    Lo now! its cradle is the old time's bier.
All realms by time must age and fade from view;
This shall through time's advance rise ever new;

2

A Nation, born in old time's drear december,
    Yet from the bosom of the Virgin May;
Stricken as fire from stone that held no ember;
    Knit as the stars are in melodious play:
Borne so to fly abroad on four-fold wings,
Heroes and poets, hierophants and kings.

3

Judgment involves by interpenetration;
    Keen, sharp, decisive is Her final thrust;
Pierces the inly quick for liberation;
    Pierces the inly dead for "dust to dust";
'Tis so the wheat is gathered from the chaff.
The planet, as a mother, thrills to laugh,

4

That now the fated labor-pains are ended,
    And the man-woman babe has crowned her bed;
He who ascended now Twain-One descended,
    On, on, to endless consummations wed;
Once to the people, in the earlier morn,
Now in a People, for deliverance born.

XCIX.

1

Bring me a cup of joy distilled from fears;
    Infuse the nectars of the holy grail.
Tears that have furrowed through me,—sorrow's tears,—
    Condensed upon my flesh to biting hail.
Clad so in piercing winter, yet it failed
To bind the Word Song; that has now prevailed.

2

Hearing, One brought a pitcher and a loaf,
    Pitcher of water, loaf of oaten bread,
Saying, "O son! drink thou and eat thereof;
    Then I will fold a mantle o'er thine head,
And thou shalt feel it as a cloud, whose veins
Open, to flow with blessings of the rains."

3

After this came to me a little sister,
    Whom I had known and loved ere mortal birth;
Christ-Christa by their lips to being kissed her;
    We were twain Word-seed in aromal earth,
And we in choral melodies were spun
Through psychic lives, ever made more at-one.

4

This is that Lily of the Morning Land,
   In whom my four-fold service ever plies;
As Lady Sue known in her household band;
   As Issa in the sacred mysteries;
Sister, muse, priestess, four-fold in the wife,
Yet named as "daughter" in the book of life.

5

"Joy-rains, joy-rains," spake she "in Lilistan!
   The land is overbrimmed with sparkling ether:
Four seasons fold in one, four skies in-span.
   As to each wedded maid, four wings enwreathe her,
Wings of the Overshadowing; they wed
From this, to form a mantle o'er thy head."

C.

1

Through interpenetration, we discern
   The end of egoized Society;
The dissolution of the civic urn,
   Leaving mankind as flowing waters free.
Not now as when the old-time deluge curled;
Then 'twas a sinking, now a rising world.

2

Wisdom has writ, in pages yet to show,
   Her record of the dying out of hells;
The rise of Word-life penetrant below;
   The bursting of the huge subversive shells;
The fourth dimensioned order opened there;
The birth and bloom of hope-time through despair.

3

Behold in Wisdom's cabinet again.
　　The door thereto is for us four-fold wide.
Here glimpse to Adonai, robed as when
　　He saw the old air-deluge overtide.
Four holy ancients here sit knee to knee.
The Word-book opens, blessed hence are we.

4

Book of the fathers, to their seed delivered!
　　Ah, childlike sit the ancients, four-fold rays
Below, above, inly and outly rivered,
　　Flow from the Ancient-Ancientess of days.
"Unfold, this leaf," spake one, mild, reverent, slow,
"Yet stand to read, girt by the vorticed bow."

5

Opens a page, in vorticed columns written.
　　Truths in the pillars rise to human height;
Truths from times past to times yet future litten,
　　Arrayed in images of Word made sight.
They may behold, inspire, achord, command,
Who inner, outer, over, under-stand.

6

In timed Eternity our thoughts awaken;
　　Within our minds four mighty pulses meet.
Deliverance shapes unto us; we are taken
　　To see where Judgment holds Her mercy seat.
Her hand has vorticed and it touches far;
Yea, from the evening to the morning star.

7

Into Her bosom She has drawn the planet;
   A babe upon Her knee, 'tis folded sweet;
For its new atmosphere Her breathings fan it;
   Earth is baptized into the Paraclete;
Star that was lost, reborn into the host
Of heaven, o'ershadowed by the Holy Ghost.

8

Into the gladness of a company
   Of blessed ones I was thereafter led;
The ladies they who were of Bethany;
   And Lazarus, whom Christ raised from the dead;
And with them others, Mary, Phœbe, Paul:
They made rich cheer as in a bridal hall.

9

The toils of nineteen centuries are ending
   For these, who led the ancient witnessing.
I felt their joy, ascending and descending,
   Inheavened in the Savior Queen and King.
To blessed close by this the Word Song drew.
Conversing yet in heaven, I bid "adieu."

THE END.

June 26—October 1, 1893.